CW01656339

PLANE DEAD

A mile-high murder puzzles Irish detectives

DAVID PEARSON

THE BOOK FOLKS

Paperback edition published by

The Book Folks

London, 2021

© David Pearson

This book is a work of fiction. Names, characters, businesses, organizations, places and events are either the product of the author's imagination or are used fictitiously. Any resemblance to actual persons, living or dead, events or locales is entirely coincidental. The spelling is British English.

All rights reserved. No part of this publication may be reproduced, stored in retrieval system, copied in any form or by any means, electronic, mechanical, photocopying, recording or otherwise transmitted without written permission from the publisher.

ISBN 978-1-913516-86-4

www.thebookfolks.com

Plane Dead is the fifth standalone title in a gripping series of mysteries set in Dublin. Details about the other books, plus a list of characters, can be found at the back of this book.

Chapter One

The European Airways flight from London's Gatwick airport to Dublin boarded without incident. It was a Friday night, just coming up to eight o'clock, with the plane due to take off at ten past the hour. All 189 seats had been sold, as was customary for this particular journey. The passengers comprised those who worked in the UK during the week and travelled home at the weekends, or were returning from a day trip to London; others who were going to Dublin just for the weekend to enjoy the 'craic', and a couple of specialist parties of 'hens' and 'stags' who had chosen the fleshpots of Temple Bar for their weekend revelry.

The mood was boisterous among many of the passengers, and the four cabin attendants – all female on this occasion – were in for a very busy time, especially as the pilot had told them that the flight time would be just 55 minutes.

At five past eight, with all 189 passengers boarded, the cabin crew closed the doors of the Boeing 737, and armed the slides as they always did before each exit was cross-checked. The pilot was informed that the cabin was secure, and the aircraft pushed back from the stand and the engines were started.

The weather on route was good, despite a little gentle turbulence as they climbed out of the southern British airport, and the atmosphere on board was lively as the stewardesses made their way slowly along the aisle serving significant quantities of alcohol to the passengers, the hen and stag parties being particularly keen to start their festivities as soon as possible.

On the flight deck, things were going smoothly. Captain Piotr Kaan, ably assisted by his Swedish co-pilot Andrea Bergin, was progressing the flight easily and steadily at 37,000 feet, crossing the Welsh border near Hereford and tracking toward Anglesey. When they reached Holyhead, they turned their machine to the west and pointed it directly at Dublin, where they would land on runway 28 into the gentle breeze.

The captain alerted the cabin staff that there was ten minutes to landing, and the drinks trollies were hastily put away while another member of the team passed through the cabin collecting empties and other rubbish in a plastic refuse sack. On this occasion, the crew had no time to sell scratch cards or reduced-price cosmetics, so heavy the demand had been for drinks on the flight.

* * *

"European 995 descend to 5,000 feet and cleared visual-ILS approach to runway 28. Wind is 260 at five knots gusting eight," the Dublin controller said.

"Roger, European 995. Down to 5,000 and cleared ILS for two-eight. Call you established."

The 737 had already captured the ILS beam that would navigate the aircraft to the threshold of the runway, although on this fine evening the flight crew didn't need its assistance. As they manoeuvred around Howth Head, they could see the strip of bright lights that was their target, coming into view.

"Landing checklist," Piotr said to Andrea who was the Pilot Flying for this leg of the journey.

"Gear down," Andrea said.

"Affirm – three greens."

"Go round alt set."

"Three thousand feet, check."

"Spoilers armed."

"Check."

"Autobrakes."

"Set to medium."

"Landing lights."

"On."

"Cabin secure, seat belt signs on."

"Check."

And when the aircraft reached 200 feet on its final approach, Piotr called out, "Minimums."

"Landing," the co-pilot responded.

As the plane glided over the threshold, Andrea closed the throttles and lifted the nose gently, allowing the big machine to flare and sink easily onto the tarmac with a puff of blue smoke from the tyres just at the touchdown point. She then rolled the reverse thrust levers up while Piotr deployed the spoilers and the machine slowly shed its momentum.

"60 knots," called Piotr and then the radio crackled into life again.

"European 995. On at 21:04. Next convenient right turn, and contact ground on 121.8."

"Next right and ground 121.8. Thanks. Bye," Piotr said into his headset.

The captain selected the second radio set which had already been programmed to the required frequency.

"European 995 with you," Piotr said.

"European 995, good evening. Follow the Bravos. Hold short of the apron. There's a company 737 just pushing back on stand 138."

"Roger, follow the Bravos and hold short for stand 138, European 995."

When the plane stopped at the end of the taxiway as directed, several passengers jumped up to retrieve their cases from the overhead lockers, anxious to get off and start partying for real. One of the flight attendants walked briskly down the aisle asking them to retake their seats and observe the 'Fasten Seat Belt' sign until they reached the gate and the captain had turned it off, while another one of the crew made an announcement to the same effect over the public address system.

After a few minutes, the departing plane was out of the way, and Andrea continued the last part of the journey, docking at stand 138 as directed, and shutting down the engines.

"Nice landing, Andrea, very smooth," Piotr said as they both completed the after-landing checklist.

"Thanks, skipper. Who's flying back to Gatwick?"

"I'll do that. There shouldn't be too much traffic at this hour. What's the booked load anyway?"

"Guess."

"Don't tell me – 189. How do they do it?" Piotr said.

"Not quite. Just 173 tonight. But there's no hurry. We're not due out till 9:55. We made good time coming across."

* * *

The senior flight attendant deployed the built-in steps at the front of the cabin, while a portable stairway was attached to the rear of the plane and the passengers slowly began to disembark. Eventually, the cabin was empty, or so they thought. But Marta, the senior cabin attendant, thought she could see a man's head protruding slightly from a window seat in row 14, so she went down along the aisle to see what was going on. Most likely, she thought, he'd fallen asleep after a few drinks. It happened quite often.

When she reached row 14, she found a man with short, mousy brown hair in a similarly coloured brown suit and a green shirt and tie slumped against the wall of the cabin. Marta leaned in across the two empty seats, and gently shook him by the shoulder.

"Sir. Sir, wake up. We are in Dublin."

There was no response, so she shook him a little bit harder, and spoke more loudly.

"Wake up, sir. We have reached our destination."

But he didn't stir.

Marta instinctively felt that there was something amiss. She had woken many passengers from a drunken slumber in her years of flying, but this was different. The man's body was limp, offering no resistance to her pushing on his upper arm and shoulder. She also noticed that there was a white substance – almost like the froth that you get when you take your first sip of beer from a glass – around his mouth.

Marta went back up to the front of the plane and summoned Captain Kaan from the flight deck.

"Captain, could you come please. We have a passenger in 14F who isn't moving, and I don't think he's asleep."

"Hmm… OK. Let me see."

Piotr Kaan sidestepped down along the aisle of the plane, following Marta's lead, till they arrived at row 14. He leaned in and placed his first two fingers against the man's neck, but could feel no pulse. The man's skin was cool and clammy too, and he had started to go an unusual blue colour around the face.

As he stood up again, he said to Marta, "I'm sorry, Marta, I think this man is actually dead."

Marta's hand flew to her face, and she started to weep as she said, "Oh my God. My God."

Kaan took Marta's arm and helped her back to the front of the plane where a European Airways despatcher in a high-vis jacket was talking to Andrea Bergin. Kaan sat Marta down and explained the situation to her colleague.

He then addressed the despatcher and told him of their dilemma.

"Jesus! Are you serious, skipper? God, I've never had anything like this before. I'd better get the duty manager. You all better stay on board for now," the man said.

"Yes, please. And you will have to get another aircraft and crew for the return flight to Gatwick. We won't be doing it," Kaan said.

"Oh, right. Yes, of course." And with that he descended the steps again and disappeared into the building.

Chapter Two

By the time Detective Inspector Aidan Burke got to the steps of the aircraft, several other Gardaí had arrived on the scene, and the aircraft had been surrounded by blue and white plastic tape to create a kind of makeshift cordon. A Garda at the foot of the stairs took Burke's name and wrote it on his clipboard, examining the senior officer's warrant card as he did so.

Burke was separated from his wife. He had married at the age of twenty-six, but by the time he reached forty, his wife, Deirdre, had become completely fed up with his constant absence and heavy drinking, and she had kicked him out. Deirdre had retained the family home in the fashionable suburbs of Knocklyon, while he just managed to keep a second mortgage going on the house in Crumlin which he had bought cheaply for himself, in poor repair. Latterly, thanks to the influence of his sergeant, Fiona Moore, he had managed to curtail his excessive use of alcohol. She had also helped him to get his house tidied up a bit, and he was no longer living in squalor. Moore had no romantic attachment to her boss, but she had a kindness in her that urged her to help a colleague who was obviously in some distress, and so far, it had worked well.

Inside the plane, crouched over the man in row 14, dressed in a white scene-of-crime suit, a woman, whom Burke assumed to be the assistant state pathologist, was probing her client gently with a long swab, collecting saliva and the frothy residue from around the man's mouth.

"Evening, Aileen," Burke said, having confirmed the identity of the woman to his own satisfaction.

Aileen Brophy stood back and turned to address Burke, whom she met regularly at the scene of some very unpleasant crimes, often involving fatalities.

"Evening, Aidan. Unusual one. Just getting started on this fellow," she said.

"What's the story?"

"By that I presume you mean what was the cause of death, and when did it occur. Patience, dear man. I've only just got here."

"Yes, but if he died of natural causes, say a heart attack, then we can all go home and I can get back to my boxed set of *CSI Miami* on my DVD player."

"You should be so lucky. Oh, yes, his heart certainly stopped beating, but then that's true in one hundred percent of human deaths, as you know. But why? He looks like a perfectly healthy man in his forties. Not overweight. Fit enough. No excess of alcohol from what I can tell. And a suspicious substance around his lips and in his mouth. If I were a guessing girl, I'd say he was most likely poisoned – but of course that's not an official opinion. You'll have to wait till we get him back to the morgue and do his bloods and toxicology for that. And that won't be till tomorrow. Sorry."

"Do we know who he is?"

"Yes. The cabin crew were able to identify him from his seat number. They think he's a Jim Farrelly, but I haven't looked for a wallet or anything. That's your job."

"OK. Thanks. How much longer will you be before we can move him?" Burke said.

"Just a few minutes. Is the van here yet?"

"Yes, I think so. It will take a good bit of pushing and pulling to get him out. I'd better send the crew inside with a couple of the Airport Police before we start that. They've had enough of a shock already."

"Do you mind if I have a look in his jacket pocket for a wallet before you remove him?" Burke said.

"Go ahead – fill your boots."

Burke donned vinyl gloves and gently felt inside the deceased's jacket, removing a wallet. He opened it and saw the man's driving licence displayed behind a clear plastic window, suggesting that he was indeed Jim Farrelly. Further exploration revealed a small stack of business cards informing Burke that he worked for a firm of solicitors with offices in Dublin, London, Paris, Frankfurt and New York. There were two Visa debit cards and a mixture of euro and sterling notes tucked in at the back as well.

* * *

Burke instructed one of the Airport Police officers to take the two pilots and four cabin crew inside and keep them in a private room until he could get a chance to come in and speak to them. He then went looking for someone from the airline, and found a rather distressed despatcher hovering in the cockpit not quite knowing what to do.

Burke introduced himself to the young man.

"I need you to find out who was sitting in the seat beside the man who died. In fact, I could do with the whole passenger list sorted by seat number if you could manage it."

"Yes, I can get that. I'll need to go into the office, but it won't take long."

"Thanks. And this aircraft will have to stay here just as it is until at least tomorrow. It may be a crime scene, so it will need to be carefully examined," Burke said.

"Can we take the baggage off?" the despatcher said.

"Yes, I don't see why not. But don't remove any of the catering or the rubbish from the plane. We'll need to examine the whole lot."

The despatcher looked a bit puzzled at this, but didn't argue.

"OK. I'll tell the ground crew. I'll go and get you that list then," he said. He was relieved to have something to occupy himself.

As Burke made his way across the apron to the terminal building, he called his sergeant.

"Is that you, Fiona?" Burke said.

"Yes, hello, boss. What's up?"

Detective Sergeant Fiona Moore was a keen young detective sergeant that Burke had spotted languishing in Pearse Street Garda station under the thumb of a lazy detective inspector who never gave her a chance. Burke had managed to get her a transfer to Store Street, and Moore's talents had blossomed under the proper guidance of the senior man. She had been instrumental in helping Burke put an end to a nasty gang that were using poorly paid port workers to smuggle narcotics into the country.

"Good evening, Fiona. I'm out at the airport. There's been a dead body found on an incoming flight from London. I need you out here to help conduct some interviews with the crew. I need Amy as well. We need to separate them to make sure their stories are consistent."

"Oh, OK. I'll get on it straight away. Meet you at the Airport Garda station?"

"Yep, fine."

In the summer months, the Airport Garda station was constantly short-handed. In any case, they were used to dealing with much more minor cases, such as a bit of roughhouse on an incoming flight, or theft from passengers' baggage. Sudden unexplained death was well above their pay grade, so they called on the City Centre Gardaí in these, very unusual, situations.

Inside the terminal Burke found the room where the European Airways crew were waiting, and he split the group up. He divided the four cabin crew into two pairs, and separated the flight crew, finding them adjoining small rooms, and asked them to be patient.

Piotr Kaan spoke up.

"It's no problem, Inspector. We're not going anywhere in any case."

Burke then went to find the European Airways despatcher that he had been speaking to earlier. He found the man in a crew room having a cup of tea and explaining recent events to his colleagues. Burke signalled him to come out into the corridor.

"What's your name, by the way? I'm Inspector Burke."

"Rory Dillon," the man replied.

"Well, Rory, I need you to organize a few things for me. I want you to make sure that that aircraft is preserved exactly as it was when it arrived – except for the baggage hold. Have you got the passenger list for me?"

"Yes, it's inside. I'll get it."

Dillon went back into the room and returned with several sheets of A4 printed paper.

"Right, thanks. Now, I want you to go and see if the passengers that were sitting in rows 13, 14 and 15 on that side of the aircraft are still in the building, and if they are, ask them to come through here and put them in another one of these rooms here."

"OK, but I have no authority to detain people."

"Well then, get help from the Airport Police. It's important that I talk to them. They may have seen something, or perhaps they were even involved."

"Cripes. OK. I'll get the airport cops to help, and don't worry about the aeroplane, I've already made those arrangements."

"Great – well done, Rory. Now, off you go."

Chapter Three

"Thanks for your patience, folks," Burke said as he went into the little room where the two flight crew were seated at a small round wooden table.

He took the third seat himself, and took out his notebook.

"Firstly, I need to have your full names and home addresses, and your mobile phone numbers," Burke said.

The two pilots provided the requested information, and Burke noted that while Kaan lived in Crawley, near Gatwick in the UK, Andrea Bergin's home was in Sweden.

"Andrea, how does that work – I mean, you living in Sweden and working out of Gatwick?"

And there it was again. That little frisson of electricity that went between them that he had first noticed when he boarded the aircraft and spoke to the flight crew. He couldn't put his finger on exactly what it was, but it was definitely there.

"It's not a problem. I have only been based in Gatwick for a few months, and I have a room near the airport. Before that, I was working out of Arlanda, so it wasn't an issue. I don't know if they will move me after this."

Burke thought that the woman's accent made her even more attractive.

"Have you been working with European Airways long?"

"Two years and a little. Before, I was with SAS. I'm a full pilot, but just now I'm working as first officer till they need a commander again."

"And you, Piotr, how long have you been with them?"

"Over five years now. I'm always based out of Gatwick. I have my family there."

"I see. So, what can you tell me about the flight tonight?"

Bergin looked at Kaan, implying that he should reply.

"Nothing odd at all, until after we landed. Andrea was Pilot Flying, and I was operating the radio and some of the equipment like the landing gear and the speed brakes. That's all normal. The wind was favourable, and they gave us a short route, so we made very good time. We shaved nearly fifteen minutes off the journey."

"Did you notice anything about any of the passengers?"

"No. We don't really interact with the passengers, except to talk over the PA. Some of them were in high spirits, but that's normal for a Friday night going into Dublin. Marta will be able to tell you more about that. She is the senior cabin attendant on the flight," Kaan said.

"Right. I believe you were due to fly back to Gatwick. What will you do now?"

"The company will put us up here as soon as you release us, and then we'll hitch a ride back to Gatwick tomorrow morning on the early flight, if that's OK?"

"Yes, that should be fine. Well, that's all I need for now. We may need you to make a statement at some stage, so please make some notes about the flight, especially around the timings, or anything at all you can remember, so that you can recall it later. Thanks for your help."

Burke handed a business card to each of them, and said, "If you remember anything unusual later, please feel free to give me a call. Sometimes it's the little, seemingly insignificant details that can be the most helpful."

"What happened to the man, Inspector?" Andrea asked.

"We don't know yet. But we're treating it as a suspicious death based on a preliminary assessment by the pathologist."

"Really! Was he injured on board?"

"I can't go into the details, Andrea, but he wasn't stabbed or anything, if that's what you mean."

"This is awful. I don't think I'll sleep a wink tonight," she said.

Burke shook hands with them both, and when Andrea took his hand, the greeting lingered a little longer than he would have expected, and her pale blue eyes twinkled brightly.

* * *

Leaving the room, Burke met Detective Sergeant Fiona Moore and Detective Amy Sutton in the corridor.

"Hi, Fiona; Amy. OK, I've spoken to the flight crew already. I need you to take two each of the cabin crew and interview them. Focus on the area around row 14 – see if they can remember what drinks they served to those passengers, and if there was anything at all unusual going on during the flight," Burke said.

As his two colleagues went off to set about the interviews, Burke saw Rory Dillon coming back down the long grey corridor accompanied by a woman in her mid-twenties dragging a pink wheelie-bag behind her.

Dillon introduced the girl as Deirdre Fagan.

"Deirdre was sitting in seat 14E on the Gatwick flight, Inspector."

"Great, thanks. Are any of the others still around?"

"No, I'm afraid not. They must have left the building already."

"OK. Is there somewhere we could have a chat?" Burke said to Dillon.

Dillon showed them to a quiet corner of the operations room which was thinning out now as the late evening flights landed and the crews came in to check themselves off duty. Burke and the woman sat at an unoccupied desk.

"Now, Deirdre, I understand you were seated beside a man in a brown suit on the flight from Gatwick. Can I ask if you had a conversation with him at all?"

"No, not really. He fell asleep more or less straight away. But I was in my seat before him, and he came along and asked me to move so that he could take his place by the window. Why? What's all this about?"

"Did you speak to him at all during the flight?"

"No, once we were sitting down, he went to sleep almost immediately. I wasn't paying much attention though. I was listening to music on my iPhone."

"So, you didn't speak to him again, then?"

"No, like I said."

"Did the man take any drinks or food from the trolley?"

"No, and neither did I. It's not terribly appetising, and quite expensive."

"I see. What happened when the plane landed?" Burke said.

"It stopped on the way to the terminal, and a few people got up out of their seats, but the cabin crew told them to sit back down. After a few minutes, the plane moved on and we arrived at the gate. Then we all got off."

"Did you notice that the man in the seat beside you hadn't moved?"

"No. I was busy getting my case down from the overhead bin. I didn't pay him any attention at all."

"OK, thanks, Deirdre. Is there anything else you can tell us at all about this?"

"I don't think so. Why? What happened to the man, in any case? He seemed perfectly normal to me."

"I'm sorry, Deirdre, but the man appears to have passed away at some stage during the flight. We're investigating the full circumstances. He may just have had a stroke or a heart attack, but we need to look into any sudden death of this nature. How come you're still at the airport anyway?"

The woman gave a gasp, and put her hand up to her face in shock.

"God! That's awful. I never knew. But my dad is collecting me – or at least he's supposed to be. He's always late!"

"OK. Well, that's all for now in any case. Can you just jot down your details on my notebook in case we need to talk to you again?"

Deirdre took Burke's pen and wrote down her name, address and mobile number.

* * *

When Burke had finished with the somewhat distraught young woman, he collected his colleagues and they made their way back to the Airport Garda station – a facility that had only recently been opened, situated at the North Terminal, the original 1950s building that had seen many iterations of refurbishment in its almost seventy years of service. When they were seated in a generous open plan area on the third floor, Burke addressed the other two.

"OK, so we now know that the dead man's name was Jim Farrelly. When we're finished here, Amy, can you get on to the bank that issued his debit card? Call the 'Lost and Stolen' card hotline and see if you can get a home address or at the very least a home phone number for the man. Don't take any of that data protection nonsense from them. Dead people are exempt."

"Yes, OK, boss."

"Did you get anything of interest from the cabin crew?" he said, addressing both of them.

Fiona Moore responded, "There was nothing unusual about the flight, apart from the fact that it was mad busy. They had to rush to get the drinks trolley all the way along the aisle before the pilot told them to secure the cabin. They said that the Friday night flights back to Dublin are always a bit crazy."

"Did the two groups tell the same story?"

"Yes. My two were working the front half of the cabin where Farrelly was seated, but they said they didn't observe anything unusual. He had his seat belt fastened for the whole flight," Moore added.

"Aren't they supposed to wake up the passengers for landing?"

"I asked them that. They said normally, yes, but it was just too busy to spot that Farrelly was still asleep, and in any case, they said that with all the noise in the cabin, they doubted whether anyone could have been really asleep. It was pretty raucous with the hen and stag parties apparently."

"Hmph, OK. Well, Amy, will you see if we can get an address for him? And then I suppose you and I better go out and break the good news to the missus, or whatever," Burke said looking at Fiona Moore.

"Right. If they are being awkward, can I call on you, sir?"

"Yes, of course, but it will be fine."

Chapter Four

Amy Sutton had managed to extract an address for Jim Farrelly from the bank's 24-hour phone banking service. It hadn't been entirely straightforward. A supervisor had to be summoned, and she had to refer to a manager, but after some delay, the man's address was provided. Sutton gave the information to Fiona Moore who, together with Burke, set off in the direction of Malahide where Farrelly lived just a few miles from the airport.

It was an upmarket area, and the address they had been given was in a small private estate of just twenty houses that had been built some eight years earlier. Although it was dark as Burke turned his Skoda Superb in through the tall pillars guarding the entrance, he could see that the place was immaculately maintained.

A few of the houses still had lights on downstairs, despite the late hour, and most of them had their numbers fixed to the piers of their own entrances, so it didn't take long for them to find number eight on the left-hand side of the curved cul-de-sac. There was a modern Mercedes parked in the driveway.

"You might have to stay here a while with his wife, depending on what state she's in. Is that OK?" Burke said to Moore.

"Yeah, I guess. Let's see how it goes."

Burke rang the bell at the front door and heard a dull ding-dong sound go off deep inside the house somewhere.

Initially, there was no reply, so he repeated his ring, and waited.

After a few minutes a shape appeared at the other side of the half-glazed front door, and it was opened. A woman, probably in her forties, with short wavy blonde hair and a round face, stood there dressed in a pink full-length towelling dressing gown with matching slippers.

"Yes?" she said apprehensively, not recognising her two late-night callers.

"My name is Detective Inspector Aidan Burke, and this is my colleague, Detective Amy Sutton. Is it Mrs Farrelly?"

"Yes, that's right. How can I help you?"

"May we come inside for a moment please, Mrs Farrelly," Moore said.

"Yes, I suppose so. What's happened? Is it Jim?"

The detectives moved forward, keen to get in off the doorstep before imparting their bad news, and Mrs Farrelly stood aside, still holding the door, but making enough room for them to enter the hallway. They stepped inside, and the woman said, "You'd better come into the drawing room," indicating a room to the left.

When they were inside the room, Mrs Farrelly invited them to sit down, and said, "It's Jim, isn't it? Has he crashed that ridiculous car of his?"

"Mr Farrelly was in the UK today, is that right, Mrs Farrelly?" Burke said.

"Yes, he left at some ungodly hour this morning for a flight. I was still asleep."

"And you were expecting him back this evening?"

"Yes, he's on the flight at around eight o'clock from Gatwick. He spoke to me earlier, and he said he was feeling quite unwell. He put it down to something he had eaten and he just wanted to get home. Inspector, what's all this about? Is Jim OK?"

"I'm sorry to tell you, Mrs Farrelly, but we believe your husband passed away during the flight back from Gatwick this evening. He was discovered unconscious in his seat when the plane landed, and our pathologist pronounced him dead at the scene," Burke said.

Mrs Farrelly sat, or more accurately, collapsed into one of the easy chairs, her hand going to her face as she started to sob loudly.

"Oh my God. Are you sure it's him?"

"We will need formal identification, but his wallet was in his jacket pocket, and the airline confirmed that he was the man seated in 14F, so we're fairly certain."

The woman sobbed quietly for a few moments into a tissue, and then recovered enough to ask, "What happened to him, officer? He's very fit, you know. And he has a medical every year for insurance purposes and he always passes with flying colours. God, I can't believe it." She resumed her tearful sobbing.

"Is there someone we can get to be with you, Mrs Farrelly?" Sutton asked.

"What. Oh, yes. My sister lives in Kinsealy. Could you call her for me and ask her to come over?"

"Yes, of course. What's her name? And do you have a number for her?"

"Sheila. Sheila Ward. She's married to Peter. And her number is in this thing," the woman said, handing Moore her mobile phone.

Fiona Moore went out into the hall to make the call.

"May I ask what your husband's occupation was, Mrs Farrelly?" Burke asked.

"He's a solicitor. He works for that big outfit down along the South Quays in the city – Milligan Walker they call it. Jim is a partner there."

"And does he travel often for work?"

"Yes. He goes to London almost every week. They have offices there in the City, just off Fleet Street. He prefers not to stay over though, so he comes back on that late flight unless he has more meetings the next day."

"What kind of work does Jim do for them?" Burke asked, deciding to keep things in the present tense to spare the woman further grief.

"They do mostly corporate work – you know, mergers and acquisitions, patents, litigation, that sort of thing. Jim has some really big international clients that he likes to look after himself."

"I see. And do you know what he was doing in London this time?"

"Not exactly. I know he had several meetings arranged. You should be able to get the details from his laptop, or from the office. I can't believe he won't be home. It's just terrible."

Fiona Moore came back into the room and said that Sheila was on her way and would be there in a few minutes.

"Could you see if you could rustle up a nice hot sugary cup of tea for Mrs Farrelly, Fiona? Thanks."

"I'm sorry to ask you, Mrs Farrelly, but we're going to need someone to identify your husband formally tomorrow. Do you think you could come in at around midday perhaps? I can have you collected so you don't have to figure out the directions if you like."

"Yes, I suppose so. Where are you keeping him?"

"There's a morgue at the airport. That's where he'll be tonight."

Fiona Moore returned with tea and three mugs that she found readily in the expansive kitchen to the rear of the property. She handed out drinks for all of them, and they sat in silence as they contemplated the situation. Their thoughts were interrupted by the doorbell, and Moore went to answer it, assuming correctly that it would be Sheila Ward.

Sheila was similar in appearance to her sister, although a little heavier, but still by no means overweight. As soon as the door was opened, she said to Moore, "Where is she? Oh my God, this is terrible."

Moore led the woman into the sitting room and she joined her sister on the sofa, putting her arms around her and joining her in heavy sobbing.

After a respectable interval, when the woman had adjusted as much as was possible to the tragedy, and was seated on the sofa comforting her sister, the detectives excused themselves and departed.

"I think that's all we can do for this evening. Why don't we get together early tomorrow and see if there have been any developments overnight? Then we can go out to Farrelly's office and have a chat with them."

"OK, boss. Sounds like a plan," Moore said.

* * *

When Aidan Burke got home, he needed a drink. He opened a fresh bottle of Jameson and poured a generous measure into one of the Waterford Crystal tumblers he had managed to retain when his marriage had broken up. As he sat there in silence sipping the warming liquor, his mind strayed back to the co-pilot of the European Airways flight.

Chapter Five

The following morning, being a Saturday, the offices of Milligan Walker were well and truly closed for the weekend, but that didn't deter Aidan Burke. When he and Fiona Moore were seated in his office in Store Street Garda station nursing a takeaway coffee apiece, he said, "I want you to get hold of the practice manager at that solicitors' place where Farrelly worked. Get him to meet us at their offices in an hour. OK?"

Moore knew better than to question her boss as to how this might be achieved, but in any case, once she got onto her computer, the firm's website soon revealed much of the information that she needed.

When she had done a bit more digging, she lifted the phone and called the number she had unearthed.

"I'd like to speak to Kendron Mitchell please. This is the Gardaí at Store Street," she said to the young man who answered the phone.

She heard the lad put down the phone and shout, "Dad, it's for you. It's the cops."

Moore could hear some shuffling and then Mitchell came on the phone.

"Kendron Mitchell, who is this please?"

Moore announced herself and said, "Mr Mitchell, we need to meet you this morning. Would you be able to come into town to your offices in, say, about forty-five minutes?"

"What's this all about, Sergeant? Our offices are closed today. It is Saturday after all, and I have a golf match this afternoon."

"I'm sorry, Mr Mitchell, I'm afraid this is quite serious, and I don't want to discuss it on the phone. Shall we say eleven o'clock?"

There was silence for a good few moments, and then Mitchell said, "Very well. If you insist. But I don't appreciate being summoned in this way, Sergeant."

"Thank you, sir, eleven o'clock then at your office."

"Bloody lawyers," she said to herself as she went back into Burke's office to relay news of their appointment.

"Thanks, Fiona. Any idea where they hang out?" Burke said.

"Oh, yes. It's one of those huge brass and glass jobs down along the South Quays. It will only take us a few minutes to get there. Let's leave at quarter to, OK?"

"Yes, fine."

* * *

Milligan Walker occupied a very impressive premises overlooking the Liffey just downriver from the well-known hostelry The Ferryman on the South Quays. The area had benefited from some serious refurbishment over the past ten years or so, and was now peppered with chic offices and various artistic endeavours that mostly occupied the old warehousing, some of which had been preserved to add atmosphere to the location.

Burke and Moore arrived outside at just after five to eleven, and spotted a serious-looking man in a navy suit getting out of a sleek, newish Jaguar outside the premises.

"That's our man, I'd wager. Let's go and say hello," Burke said, getting out of his more modest Skoda.

They approached Mitchell as he was opening the door to the offices and poking the alarm with a code to turn it off.

"Mr Mitchell? My name is Detective Inspector Aidan Burke, and this is my sergeant, Fiona Moore," he said, gesturing to his colleague.

"Well, Inspector, I hope you consider it worth your while to disturb my day off like this. This is most irregular. If it's some legal matter you want to discuss, surely that could be done during normal office hours?"

"May we go to your office please, Mr Mitchell?"

The three of them got into the glass-walled lift, and it ascended to the fourth floor giving the occupants a panoramic view of the expansive atrium beneath.

Mitchell signalled them to turn left, and a moment later they were ushered into a spacious room kitted out with ultra-modern, high-quality furniture. The office had a view out over the river through the floor-to-ceiling windows, and there was an air of freshness about the place which presumably came from the air-conditioning that pervaded the entire building.

Mitchell sat behind his expansive desk and gestured to the detectives to sit in the visitors' chairs facing him. Mitchell looked at his watch.

"Now. What's all this about? I haven't got all day you know."

"Mr Mitchell, do you have a man by the name of Jim Farrelly working with you here?" Burke said.

"Yes, of course. Jim. He's one of our more senior solicitors. He's a partner, actually. Why?"

"And was Mr Farrelly in London on business yesterday, to your knowledge?"

"Quite possibly. I don't track all of our people all of the time, but it would not be unusual. We have several international clients, and of course, we have offices in London too."

"I'm sorry to have to tell you, Mr Mitchell, but Jim Farrelly died on his flight back to Dublin last evening. We haven't had a formal identification yet, but there's no doubt that it is him."

The colour drained from Mitchell's face. "Good Lord. Are you sure, Inspector?"

"Yes, I'm afraid so. His driving licence and the contents of his wallet confirmed his identity for us. And we are treating his death as suspicious."

"Suspicious? How do you mean?" Mitchell said, looking intently at Burke.

"We believe Mr Farrelly may not have died from natural causes. Our pathologist will be conducting a post-mortem as soon as we have formal identification, but there is evidence to suspect foul play. Have you any idea why someone would want to kill one of your senior partners, Mr Mitchell?" Burke said, enjoying the moment rather more than he should have been.

"Now steady on, Inspector. Have you any actual evidence that Jim was killed? After all, wouldn't a heart attack be more like it? You can't just go around making wild statements like that without just cause."

Burke leaned forward.

"Mr Mitchell, I've been in this job for over twenty years, and I know what I'm about. Now, do I have to ask the question again?"

Moore didn't like the idea of the two men locking horns like rutting stags, so she intervened.

"What was Mr Farrelly working on just now, Mr Mitchell?"

"Just a moment. I'll look up his time recording and see," Mitchell said, awakening his PC and moving the mouse around on the desk.

"He was doing some stuff for a number of clients, but at present, he was mostly devoted to an American pharmaceutical outfit that are setting up in Ireland for tax purposes."

"And what is the name of the company, Mr Mitchell?" Moore said.

"I'm afraid I'm not at liberty to disclose that. It's a highly confidential matter. If word got out about their plans, it could scupper the whole thing."

Moore sensed that Burke was getting ready for another attack.

"Well, don't worry, Mr Mitchell, we'll probably get all we need to know from Farrelly's laptop," Moore said quickly.

"You can't do that. That's privileged information. You must return his machine to us at once. I insist!"

This time Moore wasn't quick enough.

"Wrong, Mr Mitchell. Farrelly's laptop is evidence in a potential murder enquiry, so we'll be keeping it and its contents until we find out what exactly is going on here," Burke said.

"We'll see about that, Inspector. Where is it now?"

"I couldn't possibly share that information with you, I'm afraid, Mr Mitchell. It's confidential, but rest assured, it will be quite safe," Burke said with a slight grin.

Moore interjected again.

"So, just to recap, Mr Mitchell. You are refusing to provide us with information about Mr Farrelly's clients to assist us to investigate this sorry affair. May I ask under what statute you are exercising this approach?"

"Under the statute that it's none of your damn business, that's what. Now if you'd like to leave me to it, I have some calls to make. This is extremely awkward for the firm. God only knows what repercussions it will have."

"Yes, I imagine it is. It's a bit awkward for his family too," Burke said, getting up to leave. At the door he turned back to Mitchell and said, "We'll be in touch, Mr Mitchell. And we'll see ourselves out."

When the two detectives had left, Kendron Mitchell took his mobile phone from his inside jacket pocket and dialled one of his contacts. When the call was answered, he said, “Breffni. It’s Kendron. We have a problem.”

Chapter Six

Burke walked across to the City Morgue which was located just around the corner from Store Street Garda station. He didn't enjoy post-mortems, but it was a necessary part of his job, and he had long since got over the embarrassment of throwing up, no matter how gory the specimen being carved up.

"What did you make of our Mr Mitchell then, Fiona?" he said to Moore as she struggled a little to keep up with his pace.

"Prick. And he was definitely hiding something. No, make that lots. Are you going to get a warrant to shake them up a bit?"

"Easy, tiger. All in good time. Let's see what the poor bugger died from first. He might have just croaked from some inherent problem that his annual check-up missed."

"Maybe," Moore said, not in the least bit convinced.

* * *

Dr Aileen Brophy was already togged out in her working clothes. Her hair was tied up and pushed under a blue cloth cap, and her green rubber apron covered the rest of her PPE garb.

"Hello, Inspector; Sergeant. Come in. Just about to get started on your airline passenger. But before we slice him open, I want that substance around his mouth analysed. I don't like the look of it at all."

"OK. How long will that take, Doc?" Burke asked.

"He's in no hurry. But just a few minutes. Fiachra here is a dab hand with the reagents," Brophy said, gesturing to a curly-headed young man who looked to be about fifteen to Burke.

The small group stood around the corpse of Jim Farrelly, now stripped of his business clothes, lying face up on the steel gurney with a cloth across his middle to protect whatever dignity he had left.

While the lab assistant went off to work on the swab that had been taken from the deceased's mouth, Moore said to the pathologist, "Anything interesting among his possessions?"

"Not really, just the usual. A laptop of course. It's one of those fancy Lenovo jobs made from carbon fibre. Very swish. Oh, there is one thing though. He had two phones. One was in his briefcase. It's the latest Samsung Galaxy, but the other is a cheap Nokia push-button thing and we found that in his trouser pocket. Both were turned off, so you'll need to get the techies to pop them open for you."

"Two phones! Not that unusual, I guess. He probably had one for work and the other for private use. But an old Nokia for a man who obviously enjoys the latest technology, that's a bit odd," Moore said.

After what seemed like just a few minutes, Fiachra was back, looking excited.

"You're not going to believe this, folks."

"Try me," Burke said, attempting to disguise his impatience with the additional drama which he felt was quite unnecessary.

"Ricin. Administered orally, I'd say."

"Bloody hell! Are you sure?" Burke said.

"Pretty certain, yes. I can run a few more tests, but it's not hard to detect when it's been in the system a while. But you might want to stand back from him a bit. That stuff is very deadly."

The two detectives took a pace backwards, and Fiachra offered them both a surgical mask which they donned gratefully.

"How does ricin work, Doc?" Moore said.

"Well, firstly let's confirm that it is actually ricin," Dr Brophy said. "I'll know when I open him up. If it is, his organs will all be in a bad way. His liver, kidneys, heart and lungs will all show the signs. Maybe you'd like to wait in my office. Fiachra is right, this stuff is not to be trifled with."

"Will you be long?" Moore asked.

"About half an hour should do it. If it is ricin, the damage will be extensive and very obvious. But there's something puzzling me. If he ingested the stuff then he should have been vomiting from both ends, if you see what I mean, and he would have been in great discomfort on the flight."

"OK. Well, let's see what else you can find. We'll wait in your office. Thanks."

Burke and Moore retired to the small space that was Brophy's office and sat down.

"Crikey. What do you make of that?" Moore said.

"It's weird all right. I've never encountered anything like it. You hear about these things, usually with a Russian connection, but I've never been anywhere close to it before. You?" Burke said.

"No, of course not. We need to find out how the poison works, as in how long it takes to do the job so we might be able to at least establish where it was administered," Moore said.

"Yes. Didn't the missus say that he didn't want to stay over in the UK because he was feeling a bit poorly?"

"She did. But he visits there quite often. Why don't you get on to the station while we're waiting and get them to contact European Airways for a printout of his bookings over the past three months. Might as well check with Aer Lingus too, although it looks as if he was a European Airways fan," Burke said.

Almost as soon as Fiona Moore had finished setting things up with her colleagues in Store Street, Dr Brophy came into her office.

"Well, it looks like Fiachra was right. His internal organs were rightly buggered up, and the damage fits with ricin. His liver, pancreas and gastrointestinal tract are all badly damaged. That's typical of the poison after it's been ingested. But I think you said the passenger sitting beside him said he was asleep during the flight, is that right?"

"Yes, that's what she said, though I don't think she was paying him much attention. She was listening to music on her phone. Why?"

"Well, if he was in the latter stages of ricin poisoning, I'd expect some writhing about, maybe even fitting. So, he may have had something else in him too. I'll get a full tox report done as soon as we can. That will tell us."

"How long does ricin take to work, Doc?" Moore asked.

"A very good question, Sergeant. The problem is that it varies hugely. In some cases, it could be as quick as a few hours. In others, symptoms can take some days to develop, especially if the dose was small. It's impossible to tell with Mr Farrelly when he took it, I'm afraid."

"And what does ricin look like anyway? Surely, he would have known what was happening? How much do you reckon he received?" Burke said.

"Well, firstly, very little of the stuff can cause death. It's very toxic. For a man of his proportions, I'd say 90 milligrams would have been enough to see him off. And before you ask, that's about the size of a standard paracetamol tablet. If you wanted it to act a bit more slowly, 50 milligrams may have been given. It would in all likelihood have the same effect, just over a longer period of time," Brophy said.

"Crikey, I see what you mean about deadly. And where do you get that stuff anyway? It's hardly available over the counter at Boots," Moore said.

"That's up to you to find out. But you're right, it's not easy to get hold of in tablet form for obvious reasons, but it's not hard to make it at home. And I imagine it could be had on the dark web, but I'm just guessing."

"Terrific. Remind me never to ask you for a headache pill, Doctor!" Burke said.

Aileen Brophy was not amused.

"Right. Well, let's get out of here, Fiona. Thanks for your help, Doc. Before we go, is there any way that you can determine the origin of the poison for us? That would be a big help."

"No, sorry. It's all infused in his system now. We won't be able to separate the toxin from the rest of him at this point. But if anything does occur, I'll let you know. And you'll have my report by first thing tomorrow, but the toxicology will take a bit longer. If I was to guess, I'd say he was given a sedative with the poison. That would account for the drowsiness on the flight. If that is the case, then you're looking at a very sophisticated operation indeed."

"Terrific! Thanks anyway, we'll talk soon."

Burke and Moore walked back to Store Street in silence, each one of them trying to figure out a scenario that could have seen a prominent Dublin solicitor murdered in such an horrific way. What could be behind it? Was it something in his private life that caught up with him so dramatically, or was it more likely connected to his work? Questions, questions, and so far, at least, no answers – none at all.

Chapter Seven

"Coffee, boss?" Moore said when they arrived into work on the following Monday.

"Yes, thanks, Fiona, and make it strong," Burke said.

He sat down at his desk and started doodling on a page of his jotter.

When Moore came back with two mugs of strong coffee, she said to Burke, "What now, then?"

"As I see it there are two possibilities at this point. One, he may have been playing away and got himself entangled with the wrong types. If he was sleeping with a Russian woman in London, say, God knows who she might have been connected to. Or, two, it's work-related. What do you think?"

"My money is on the work. Even if he was having an affair, he should have been old enough and wise enough to steer clear of that kind of trouble. And we have no idea what he was working on, and I can't see Kendron Mitchell volunteering too much information. What kind of name is that anyway – Kendron? Sounds like something out of Downton Abbey," Moore said.

"Yes, I agree. It's a weird one. But you know what some of these law firms are like. I spotted in the foyer that the practice was established in 1941, so his father, and maybe even his grandfather could have been there before him. Anyway, enough of that. Here's what I propose. Tomorrow, I'll go back to the solicitors' office and give our Kendron a real shake-up. I want you to go calling on the wife. Take Dónal Lawler with you, but you lead. Find out if she's really as upset as she seemed when we broke the news to her. Poke around a bit. See what you can shake loose."

"OK. But be careful, boss. You know what this lot are like. They'll have some connections further up the food chain if I know anything, and they could try and tie us up in knots with legalities of one kind or another," Moore said.

"They can try. But you're right. Maybe I'll go upstairs and have a word before we go in all Starsky and Hutch. Oh, and can you get the tech lads working on his laptop and phones? They'll probably tell us more than Mitchell anyway."

"Good idea."

* * *

Jerome Heffernan was a Cork man who had been obliged to come to Dublin to accept promotion to superintendent when there were no suitable vacancies in the Southern Division of the Gardaí. He was a cunning man, and was considered to be a safe pair of hands with some of the more sensitive cases that arose in central Dublin. He had managed a nasty business involving espionage and drug smuggling from China very successfully, where an airport worker had been killed, and was therefore generally left largely to his own devices by the Assistant Commissioner. But he well aware that each new case had its pitfalls, and if any of his subordinates were to slip up badly during the pursuit of their quarry, he would soon get it in the neck from on high.

Burke knocked on Heffernan's door.

"Ah, come in, Aidan. What can I do for you?" the superintendent said from behind a large mahogany desk that was positioned against the far wall of his spacious, carpeted office.

"Good morning, sir. I just wanted to bring you up to date on the man that was found dead out at the airport on Friday night."

Burke went on to outline what they knew so far, and gave a glimpse of his plans for the following day, without going into too much detail.

"God, Aidan, go carefully, will you? These fancy lawyers are often well connected. What did you say the practice manager was called?"

"Mitchell, Kendron Mitchell, sir."

Burke noticed that Heffernan was writing down the name in his daybook. No doubt, as soon as Burke had left, the senior man would start his own investigation into the firm of Milligan Walker.

"I can't say I've heard of him, but that doesn't mean he can't pull a few strings on us. And that sounds like a very elaborate way to see someone off. Are you sure this Farrelly fella didn't just get a dodgy oyster and a bad pint in one of those fancy London restaurants?"

"Certain, sir. The pathologist was quite positive in her diagnosis of the cause of death," Burke said.

"Well, I'll be damned. I never came across the like of that in all my time. But with a bit of luck, we'll find out the poison was administered in London and we can hand the whole thing over to the Met. I'm not sure we have the capability to be dealing with this kind of thing here."

"Possibly, sir. But I'd like to continue with our investigation in any case and see where it leads us."

"Of course, but you can see where I'm coming from, Aidan. Let's not make an international incident out of this if we can help it. That doesn't go down too well in The Park these days, what with the squeeze on resources and everything."

"Yes, I see what you mean. Will that be all, sir?"

"Yes, for now in any case, but keep me posted, and I'll let you know when the flak starts flying, as I'm sure it will."

"Thanks." Burke got up and left the superintendent to it.

Heffernan probably realized that the interview he had just had with his inspector would have the exact opposite effect. Burke would be even more determined to get to the bottom of the case than he had been before he saw the senior man, and Heffernan knew it.

"I'd better start building our defences," he said to himself when Burke was gone, "this is going to be one hell of a ride."

Little did he know just how right he was.

Chapter Eight

"C'mon, Fiona, let's go," Burke said, steaming through the open plan office at a jaunty pace.

"OK, boss, where to?" she said, hurriedly grabbing her jacket from the back of the chair and her mobile phone off the desk. She just about had time to lock her PC screen, knowing that any failure to do so would result in a yellow slip from the sergeant who regularly patrolled the office to see that protocols were being observed.

As they emerged into the car park, Moore tried again.

"Where are we going, boss?"

"Just get in, Fiona. It's not far."

Burke drove quickly out across the river and down along the south quays, pulling up with a jerk outside the offices of Milligan Walker. He turned to his colleague. "Happy now?"

"Delirious," she replied, following his lead and getting out of the vehicle.

Inside at the reception desk, Burke demanded to see Kendron Mitchell.

"I'll just check to see if he is available," the receptionist said, trying not to show the intimidation she felt from the inspector.

Burke turned away and looked out across the river, but both his sergeant and the receptionist could feel the impatience radiating from him.

"Mr Mitchell is in a meeting, sir, but he said to say that he will be free in about fifteen minutes if you'd like to take a seat. Maybe I could arrange a coffee?" she said, hopefully.

"I haven't got fifteen minutes to spare, and I don't want a bloody coffee, so could you call him back and get him down here please – now!"

The poor girl returned to the relative sanctuary of the phone, and relayed the message to Mitchell's PA. After a bit of back and forth with Mitchell's assistant, the receptionist hung up and said, "Mr Mitchell will be down directly, sir."

Burke just grunted, and strolled over to the comfy-looking sofa at the other side of the atrium and took a seat.

Moore looked at the beleaguered receptionist and just shrugged, indicating her sympathy for the girl without saying anything.

* * *

Mitchell appeared a few moments later, somewhat flustered. He came out through the turnstiles into the reception area and walked over to where Burke was seated.

"Good day, Inspector; Sergeant. This really is most inconvenient. I was in a–"

But he never got a chance to finish his sentence, because Burke, standing up, cut across him.

"Mr Mitchell. I don't give a rat's ass how inconvenient this is for you. I'm investigating the murder of one of your senior partners, and in case you don't ever read detective stories or watch them on TV, the police have the best chance of catching the perpetrator within a few days of the act itself. So, I need to ask you some questions, inconvenient or not. Got it?"

Mitchell muttered something under his breath, but neither of the Gardaí could hear it, which was probably just as well. He turned and walked off towards the turnstile that gave access to the offices above, and Burke and Moore followed.

When they were once again seated in Kendron Mitchell's office, Burke commenced his enquiries.

"Right, Mr Mitchell, I need a full list of Jim Farrelly's clients here at the firm. I'd like you to go back eighteen months, and I'd like the complete files on anything that he was dealing with currently – that's everything, no matter how trivial it may seem. OK?"

Mitchell shuffled uneasily in his seat.

"I'm afraid that is completely out of the question, Inspector. As you know, those files are protected by the general rules of client confidentiality between an organisation and its legal representatives, and in any case, we are constrained by the GDPR protocols from disclosing personal data in any form."

Mitchell sat back with a slightly smug countenance.

"It seems, oddly, Mr Mitchell, that you are not as familiar with the GDPR protocols to the extent that I would have expected. Recital 27 of the regulation determines that deceased persons are no longer protected by the GDPR, and as it seems that much of Mr Farrelly's work involved UK clients, and the UK is no longer a member of the European Union, then the GDPR cannot be applied to those files either. So, perhaps you would be good enough to ask someone to get them together for us, and while we are waiting, I have a few more questions."

"No, Inspector. I won't be doing that. The entire basis of our relationship with our clients is one of trust and confidentiality. If I were to do as you ask, that trust would be broken, and we might as well all pack up and go home. So, I'm sorry, but I cannot agree to your request."

"I see. Well first of all, Mr Mitchell, it's not a request. And secondly, my sergeant here will now return to Store

Street where she will ask the superintendent to prepare a warrant. When that is ready, some thirty or so uniformed Gardaí will arrive here in squad cars and start combing out every drawer, every PC, every wastepaper basket, every nook and cranny of this place till we get all that we need. If that's the way you want to play things, then that's all fine by me."

Burke turned to Fiona Moore.

"Off you go, Fiona. I'll wait here."

As Moore got up to go and do her boss's bidding – she still wasn't sure if he was bluffing or not – Mitchell said, "Wait."

The man got up from his seat and walked around, opening the door of his office and gesturing to the two detectives to follow him.

The three walked in convoy down along the glass-lined corridor, past several offices with people inside, talking on the phone or tapping quickly on keyboards. Others were in deep discussions with colleagues or clients. It was a busy place.

They turned left at the end of the corridor, and Mitchell took a set of keys off his belt where they had been attached. He selected a key and opened an office which was empty, but had the name 'Mr J Farrelly' stencilled on an aluminium plate placed discreetly beside the door.

Mitchell ushered Burke and Moore into the office.

"This is, sorry was, Jim's office. His files are all here, and his cabinet isn't locked. I'll get his PA to sit in with you while you rummage amongst his things. Please don't leave the place in a mess." With that he turned and departed.

Burke sat in behind the desk and swivelled the chair around so that he was looking straight out across the river at the newly built Convention Centre and the myriad of new offices that had been built all along the quayside.

"I could get used to this," he said to Moore, who was a bit embarrassed at the cheek of her colleague, and not for the first time that day.

A moment later and a neatly dressed, slim woman with dark hair cut in a bob entered the room.

"I'm Miriam Clarke. I'm Jim's PA. Not exclusively of course, I work for two other solicitors here too. How can I help?"

Moore shook hands with the woman, and Burke, sensing her discomfort at seeing him seated where her boss used to be, got up and came round to the front of the desk.

"Hello, Miriam. I'm very sorry for your loss. It must have come as a dreadful shock to you. Have you worked with Jim for a long time?" Burke said.

"Yes, I suppose so. It must be four years now. He was a nice man. He could be determined when the situation called for it, but underneath he was a gentle man, in the true sense of the word."

Moore felt that the woman was choosing her words carefully. What exactly did 'determined' mean in a work context, she wondered.

"Miriam, rather than starting to go through all these files ourselves, maybe you could tell us a bit about Mr Farrelly's work at the moment. Who were his current clients?" Moore said.

"Well, recently he's been pretty tied up with a pharmaceutical company, AMRAAL Incorporated which is based in the USA. But he has other clients on the go as well. Fintrade is another one he does work for. They are a factoring outfit that provide managed cashflow solutions for heavy industry, as far as I know. But I don't really know the ins and outs of his work. I just do the correspondence, emails and billing, of course," Miriam said.

"AMRAAL. That's an odd name. What does it stand for?" Burke asked.

"I think it's American Medical Research Analysis and Licensing, or something like that. They want to set up an Irish operation to manufacture one of their patented medicines. I think it's mostly about tax, but I'm no expert," Miriam said.

"And is that what Jim was doing in London?" Moore said.

"Yes, well partly at least. He was also working with our London firm on some other clients. He had a lot of valuable experience to offer, and they were glad to have his help."

"I see. And who in your London office was his main contact?" Burke said.

"That would be Breffni Wagstaff. It's not a big operation over there. They have some valuable clients; it's quite a small office, but growing."

"So, Miriam, can you tell us roughly how much Jim charged for his time and expertise?"

"Do you think it's OK to divulge that information? It's kind of confidential," the woman said, clearly uneasy with the question.

"Well, it will be in his files in any case, but it would be quicker if you just told us," Burke said.

"His normal charge out rate was €2,000 an hour, but of course he didn't bill every hour that he was here. Just when he was in meetings or working on a report or a proposal, or filing returns for a client or whatever."

"Wow! Nice work if you can get it," Moore said, and immediately regretted the comment.

"Do you think so?" Miriam said, coolly.

"Sorry, I didn't mean to be glib. How does all that work anyway? Does the fee all go to the practice or what?"

"No. Each of the partners, and the more junior solicitors, are more or less self-employed. They keep their own fees, and then the management committee levy them for rent and other costs associated with running the practice like establishment costs, insurance, training costs for the juniors and so on. The juniors pay a smaller levy, and the partners who have more earnings pay more. It's a model that is quite widely used among large law firms as far as I am aware."

"And does that all work smoothly?" Burke asked.

"Well, sometimes there is a bit of a scrap, especially if the charges are going up a lot. But they usually settle it amicably enough over a few bottles of wine," she said, smiling.

"How often do these meetings take place?"

"Twice a year. There's one main budget meeting in November for the following year, and then a mid-term meeting for adjustments if any are required."

"OK, Miriam. Perhaps you could dig out the files on AMRAAL and Fintrade for us. Just go back about three months, and we may have to come back to look at Jim's PC, so please make sure no one interferes with it, and keep the door locked," Burke said.

"He doesn't have an office PC other than his laptop. That's just a screen you see there. It's not connected to anything. That's the way we all work. It means he can take it to London or wherever and have all his stuff with him. He just connects it to the network in London, and he can see all his files and emails. Did you take that away from the aeroplane?"

"Yes, we did. Our forensic team have it now, along with his mobile phones. There may be some clue amongst all that as to why he died," Burke said.

"OK. So, we'll just nip out and get a coffee while you are collecting up the files. We'll be back in half an hour or so. Is that OK?" Moore said.

"Yes, fine. I'll leave them in reception for you."

Chapter Nine

Back at the Garda station, Burke had given Moore the task of going through the files that they had collected from the solicitors' offices.

"Oh, and when you get a minute, give forensics a call about his laptop and phones, will you? I'm sure they have some useful stuff on there," Burke said.

Moore felt a bit miffed being dumped on. It would take a good while to explore the files that Miriam had given them, and she was wondering what Burke was going to do with his time. She decided to call forensics first.

"Hi, Daniel, this is Fiona here. I was wondering if you have had a chance to crack open Jim Farrelly's laptop. The boss is keen to get inside it and see what it can tell us."

"Oh, right. Yes, I'm sorry, Fiona, but there's a problem with that. It has a BIOS password set on it, and if we don't know what that is, the laptop is locked up tight. Could you call his office or his wife or someone and see if you can get hold of it?"

"Can you not just try a few obvious things? It can't be that hard."

"No dice, I'm afraid. It's a ThinkPad, so there's probably a hard drive password on it too. If I try too many times, I'll be locked out for good."

"OK, I'll see what I can do."

Moore called Miriam again, but the woman was unable to help.

"I'm sorry, Sergeant, the partners each keep their own passwords. They're not written down anywhere or anything, and I have no idea what Jim might have used," Miriam said.

"OK, thanks," Moore said, and ended the call.

She tried Mrs Farrelly, and unfortunately got the same result. She wasn't looking forward to telling Burke the bad news given the humour he was in.

* * *

Burke dialled the number that Andrea Bergin had given him when they met on the fateful evening. He assumed she would probably be somewhere above Europe at 37,000 feet at this time of day, but he hoped she would have a voicemail on her phone. He was right.

"Hi, Andrea. It's Inspector Aidan Burke here from Ireland. I wonder if you could call me back when you get this message? It's nothing urgent, but I need a word when it's convenient for you. Thanks."

When he had finished the call, he went in search of Fiona Moore who was just getting to grips with the files.

"What's the story on Farrelly's laptop, Fiona?"

Moore told him what Daniel had said, and that she hadn't had any luck getting the password from either the office or his wife.

"For fuck's sake! Call this a modern-day police service. Who is looking after it in forensics?"

"That's Daniel. I think he's doing his best."

Burke lifted the phone on Moore's desk and called Daniel.

"Daniel? It's Inspector Burke here. What's all this nonsense about not being able to get into Farrelly's laptop?"

"That's right, sir. Its password-protected, and we can't find or guess the password."

"Christ, Daniel, surely we can't be stumped by a simple password!"

"It's not simple, sir. IBM have made these laptops very secure, which is why corporate customers like to use them."

"But there must be a way around it."

"There is, sir, but you're not going to like it," Daniel said.

"Go on."

"You have to replace the BIOS chip on the motherboard. I'd have to buy one off a dodgy supplicr on eBay, and then assuming it comes in OK, I'd have to use a soldering iron to remove the existing one, and solder in the new one which would have no password on it."

"Bloody hell. And what would all that cost?"

"It's not expensive. Around €30 or thereabouts. It's just a bit tricky."

"Are you sure there's no other way?"

"Yes, sir, positive."

"OK. Do it! And try and get the chip thingy couriered to us if you can, to speed things up."

"I don't think that will be necessary, sir. I think I can probably get one locally and collect it. So, I might have the thing opened up tomorrow. Would that be OK, sir?"

"Excellent, Daniel, good man. What about the phones?"

"That's a lot easier. I'll have that downloaded later today and I'll send you a transcript of everything on them."

"Great, you're a star. Thanks."

"There you are, you see, problem solved," Burke said to Moore, who just smiled back at him and returned to the paperwork.

* * *

Burke was sitting at his desk where he had a large chicken salad sandwich and a cardboard carton of vegetable soup for his lunch. He was just about to get stuck in when his phone rang. He looked at the screen, but didn't immediately recognize the number.

"Burke," he said rather impatiently into the instrument, thinking that his meal would be getting cold.

"Inspector Burke. This is Andrea Bergin here. I got a message to call you."

"Oh, yes, Andrea. Thanks for ringing. I presume you were flying when I called earlier."

"Yes. Always the same routine. Monday and Wednesday it's Gatwick–Tenerife. Tuesday and Thursday we do Gatwick–Las Palmas and Friday it's two, or sometimes three, Dublins. This evening we had a bad storm over Biscay, so we were a bit delayed. How can I help you?"

"Does flying through bad weather bother you, Andrea?"

"No, not a bit. This evening Piotr was PF, so I was just sitting there getting shaken up and trying to calm the passengers. But it's fine. Less boring for us in any case."

"PF, sorry I don't recognize the term."

"Sorry, that's Pilot Flying. It means he is in charge of the flight. We do one leg each as PF, and I flew down today."

"Oh, right, rather you than me. Anyway, you remember I said we might ask you back to make a statement about the evening Mr Farrelly died on board? Well, I was wondering if you would perhaps like to do that on Friday when you are in Dublin? I could come to the airport to meet you if you like," Burke said, all thoughts of dinner now forgotten.

"Yes, of course. In fact, I was thinking of maybe staying over in Dublin one of these weekends. I could come in as a passenger on that last Gatwick flight. I'd like to see some of the city. I believe it's a nice place."

"Yes, that's a good idea. Perhaps we could have a meal together, or maybe you would allow me to show you around on the Saturday?"

"That would be lovely, thank you. Could you recommend a hotel for me? The one at the airport is very expensive. I'd need somewhere a bit cheaper and nearer town."

Burke thought carefully for a moment.

"Look, Andrea, I know this is a bit forward of me, but I have a spare bedroom here at my place. It's not luxurious, but it is cheap! Would you like to stay here? No funny business, of course. Just somewhere for you to sleep."

There was a silence which Burke felt went on for rather longer than he would have liked, but he stayed quiet until she responded.

"That's very kind of you, Aidan. Yes, I'm sure that would be fine, and dinner is on me, OK?"

"Deal!" Burke said with great relief. "I'll collect you off the Gatwick flight on Friday. I'm looking forward to seeing you again, Andrea."

"Yes, me too. Till Friday, then. Bye."

Chapter Ten

Fiona Moore continued to pore over the paperwork that they had taken back from Farrelly's office. There was a lot of it. Much of it related to the American pharma company, AMRAAL. There were copies of application forms for grant aid from the IDA, abridged accounts that had been notarised by the solicitors, and endless correspondence reporting progress, or in some cases, lack of it, between Farrelly and the company's head office in Raleigh, North Carolina. Raleigh was apparently a hub for a number of pharmaceutical companies, including many of the big brand names.

There was reference in the documents to two specific medicines that AMRAAL were hoping to manufacture in Ireland. Panidrox, a general-purpose analgesic composed mainly of paracetamol, but with some added ingredients to make it more effective, and a drug called Trebutivan which was for the treatment of kidney disease. There was very little information about Trebutivan. Its formulation was seemingly a closely guarded secret, and it had only recently been given approval by the FDA in the US.

As Moore read on, she discovered that Trebutivan, in tablet form, would cost the patient, or their healthcare provider, several thousand US dollars a month, which made it potentially one of AMRAAL's big earners. The other product would be an 'over-the-counter' product, and hence would have to compete with several other similar medicines already established in the market.

But there was nothing in any of the files that gave any clue as to why anyone would have wanted to do away with Jim Farrelly. It all seemed entirely straightforward, if a little overworked and laborious. Neither was there any indication as to whether AMRAAL were close to setting up in Ireland, although Moore figured that they probably weren't too far away from it, based on what she had read.

Fed up with what seemed like a fruitless task, Moore decided to change tack. She retrieved the notes that she and Amy Sutton had taken when she was interviewing the cabin crew on the night Farrelly was discovered. There were four females looking after the flight. Marta, the senior stewardess, assisted by an English girl, Sally, and two other Eastern European attendants: Elena who was originally from Romania, and Nikolina who was from Bulgaria.

They had all testified that the flight was extremely busy, as was the norm for a Friday night journey from the UK to Dublin. Marta had supervised the loading of the catering at Gatwick, which consisted mostly of drink with a few sandwiches and snacks, and had signed off the chit to confirm the delivery. There was nothing unusual about the flight at all, they confirmed, and they were all looking forward to a quieter journey back to Gatwick.

Marta and Sally had manned the forward section of the cabin, and the other two girls looked after the passengers further aft. As was customary, they started the service from the first and last rows respectively, and met near the centre of the cabin just before the captain announced ten minutes to landing when they had to put their trollies away for the arrival. Marta confirmed that some passengers right in the middle of the plane never actually got served, such was the duration of the flight, and there had been a bit of moaning from them, but nothing untoward. Moore noticed that row 14 was one of the rows not to have been included in the in-flight service.

* * *

Burke emerged from his office in much better form than earlier, and gathered his team around for an update.

"Fiona. What did you get from the files? Anything useful?" he said.

"Not really, boss." She went on to relate what she had discovered about AMRAAL and their plans.

"Is that it? What about the other clients Farrelly was working with?"

"I haven't got to them yet, boss. It's a slow process."

"Evidently. OK, keep at it. Anything else to excite us, Amy?"

"No, I'm afraid not, sir. I did go back over the statements given by the flight attendants, but it all seems very ordinary."

"How long did the pathologist say that this shit takes to act?" Burke said.

"She was vague about that. A few hours to a few days, if I remember correctly. Why?" Amy Sutton said.

"Well, it was obviously given to him unbeknownst. So, check out if it was the same flight crew on his outward journey. Find out what seat he was sitting in on the morning flight, and who was seated next to him. Then let's re-interview the cabin attendants about the Dublin–Gatwick flight as well."

"Right, boss."

"Also, I'd like you to get a full passenger list from both flights and start going through our PULSE system and the Europol database and see if we get any hits. And I'd better open up a channel with our British brethren. If Farrelly was got at on the morning flight, or while he was in London, they'll want to be involved," Burke said. "I'll start with their London office."

"But, sir, it will still be our case, won't it, even if there is a UK involvement?" Amy Sutton said.

"Let's see, Amy, but yes, I imagine so. We have the body after all," he said grimly.

* * *

When Aidan Burke called the London office of Milligan Walker, it was answered by an operator with an educated British accent.

"Milligan Walker, Sarah speaking, how may I help you?"

"This is Inspector Aidan Burke of the Irish police. I'd like to speak with Breffni Wagstaff please."

"Just one moment, sir," the girl said, and the phone started to emit soothing jazz music.

She was back a moment later.

"I'm sorry, sir, Mr Wagstaff has left for the day. May I take a message?"

"Could you give me his mobile number please?"

"I'm sorry, sir, we are not allowed to give out mobile numbers for our staff. But I can take a message if you like?"

"Can you connect me to his PA then?" Burke said, becoming a little impatient.

"I'm sorry, sir. Miss Denham has also left for the day."

"Right! Well, here is what I want you to do, Sarah. I want you to call Wagstaff on his mobile phone, give him my number, and say I'd like him to call me within the next half hour. It's important. Can you do that?"

"I'll try, sir, but he may have turned off his phone. May I have your number, sir?"

Burke reeled off his mobile number remembering to put 00353 in front of it.

"In that case you can call his home, his golf club, his favourite watering hole, Miss Denham and anyone else you can think of until you locate him. I'd hate to have to ask the Metropolitan Police to find him for me. OK?"

"I'll do what I can, sir."
"Thank you, Sarah. Goodbye."

Chapter Eleven

Burke was alone in the pub enjoying his second pint of Guinness when his phone began to chirp in his pocket.

"The elusive Mr Wagstaff, no doubt," he said to himself, withdrawing the device from the inside pocket of his jacket.

"Burke," he said when he had answered it.

"Hi, boss, it's me. Where are you?"

"Oh, hello, Fiona. I'm in Mulligan's having a pint before I head home. Why?"

"I think you might want to come back to the station, sir. It's Mrs Farrelly. She's been involved in a bad car accident on the back road between Malahide and Portmarnock."

"Shit! Is she OK?"

"I'm not sure, sir. The first responder recognized her car and made the connection to her husband and called us. But he didn't say how badly injured she is."

"Right, I'm on my way. I'll see you in the car park. We'd better get out there – and you're driving."

"OK."

Burke downed the remainder of his drink in one go, and left to walk the short distance back to Store Street Garda station.

* * *

Moore drove out at maximum speed towards Portmarnock. She took the coast road as far as the Baldoyle Road where there were fewer junctions and sets of traffic lights to slow her down, and then she turned off, up past the DART railway tracks and out along the coast road from Baldoyle church. Then she turned inland again to go up towards St Olave's and past the driving range, finally pulling up at the blue 'road closed' sign that had been put across the carriageway on the way into Portmarnock.

The scene was fairly chaotic. A fire tender with its blue lights flashing was inside the cordon slewed across the road blocking it completely. Beyond that, the mangled wreckage of Mrs Farrelly's car could be seen partially on its side, and fluids of all kinds were seeping out of it onto the road surface. The vehicle was still steaming, and one of the firemen had an extinguisher at the ready in case it burst into flames.

Burke spoke to the uniformed Garda who was manning the closure.

"What's the story here, Guard?"

"It happened about thirty minutes ago, sir. This chap over here in the red Toyota was going towards Portmarnock when the other car came careering round under the bridge at huge speed and whacked into the stonework before tipping up and hitting the pole and the bank."

"How many occupants of the crashed vehicle?"

"Just the one, sir, a woman."

"Did she survive?"

"The guys from the fire tender are working on her now, but it doesn't look good. I haven't been over. I've been busy managing the traffic."

"OK, thanks," Burke said, ducking underneath the blue and white tape and walking towards the wreckage.

The woman who was driving the crashed car was still inside. The airbags had all gone off, and the inside of the car was covered in white dust. A paramedic was leaning in trying to see if the woman could be freed from her car without doing further damage.

Moore spoke to the other fireman who was standing by with cutting gear in case it should be needed.

"Is she going to make it?" Moore said.

"I'm afraid she hasn't. I'd say it was instant. According to the driver of the Toyota, she came round the bend like a bat out of hell. It's a strong car, but nothing could protect you in that situation. The bridge is solid granite."

Moore was always surprised that the men who manned fire engines in Dublin were medically trained. The ambulance crews and the fire crews were interchangeable in the Dublin Fire Brigade, providing double cover in these kinds of situations.

It took another forty minutes to extricate Mrs Farrelly from what remained of her car. An ambulance had arrived, and after death had been confirmed, she was loaded onto a trolley, covered from head to toe in a sheet, and placed in the ambulance which set off at a gentle pace for the city morgue. When they had departed, Moore donned vinyl gloves and went to examine the car.

It was a mess. Barely recognisable, but in the strange way that these things work, parts of the car looked hardly touched at all by the accident. She found the woman's handbag on the floor in what had been the passenger footwell, picked it up, and put it into an evidence bag. There was a dashcam attached to the crazed windscreen just beside the rear-view mirror. Moore leaned in, being careful not to catch her clothes or her skin on the jagged metal edges that had appeared as the car disintegrated, and popped the little SD card out from the side of it. She put that in a smaller plastic bag and stuffed it into her pocket. She had a look around the interior. There was nothing else of note. A few receipts in the pocket of the driver's door, now hanging off its hinges at a crazy angle, and some coins for parking that had been in the centre console and were now scattered around everywhere.

She exited the wreckage, took some photos on her phone making sure to get the number plate in a couple of them, and went back to where Burke was talking to the driver of the red Toyota. The man was clearly in shock. He was in his late fifties, and looked to be a tradesman by the nature of the clothes he was wearing. He had been on his way home from a job in Baldoyle when he happened upon the scene.

"A few seconds later, and she would have hit me head-on," he said, shaking his head. He had little to say, except that the woman was driving much too fast for the road. He didn't really see much. He was too busy trying to avoid getting hit by the careering car to make any significant observations.

"Righto, well thanks anyway. Are you OK to drive?" Burke said to the man, not really having any clue as to what to do if he answered in the negative.

"Yes, I'll be fine. Just give me a few minutes to pull myself together. I'll have to turn the car and go back up by Kinsealy, I suppose."

"Yes. This road will be closed for the rest of the night. Our forensics people will be along shortly to take observations, measure the skid marks and so on. It should be open again by the morning," Burke said.

As if on cue, the Forensic Collision Investigation team arrived and started doing their stuff. They chalked the road where the car had come to rest, and made several notes at both sides of the bridge that Mrs Farrelly had struck. They took a lot of photographs to document the gruesome scene.

Burke turned to Moore and said, "I suppose someone will have to go out and tell the sister. Have you still got her phone number?"

"Yes, I think so. Ward, wasn't it? Sheila Ward?" Moore said.

"Yes, that's her. As we only have one car between us, I suppose we'd better go together then," Burke said.

Moore was glad she didn't have to do that awful job all on her own.

Chapter Twelve

They found Sheila Ward's house easily enough. It was a spacious property, detached, and sitting on what must have been at least an acre of well-tended grounds. The S-shaped drive up to the house was guarded by tall wrought-iron gates with an intercom arrangement for visitors. As Moore pulled off the road, her car facing the gates, Burke got out and went to the device attached to the pillar that was emitting a pale blue light.

He pressed the bell push, and a few moments later it was answered by the woman that they had summoned to Jim Farrelly's house just a few days previously to comfort her sister, who by now would be on her way to the morgue to join her husband.

"Mrs Ward, it's Detective Inspector Burke here with Sergeant Moore. I wonder if we could come in for a few minutes?"

Sheila Ward didn't reply, but the gates gave a loud clunk, and slowly started to open backwards into the garden of the house.

Burke rejoined his colleague, and as they drove up the gravelled driveway, the gates swung slowly closed behind them.

The house was a double-fronted dormer construction, with what must have been sizeable rooms on both sides of the hallway. Four windows were set into the shingled roof, and to the side, a large double garage with a separate pitched roof was located. On the other side of the house, across well-manicured lawns, a wooden summer house painted in pale green completed the picture.

"Nice place. I wonder what Mr Ward does?" Moore said.

"Whatever it is, he does it well by the looks of things. Tenner bets he's a lawyer or a medical consultant," Burke said.

"Na, you're OK. Probably right at that."

Mrs Ward had opened the front door, and was standing in the entrance looking apprehensive.

The two detectives got out and went over to her.

"What brings you here at this time of night? I was just getting ready for bed," the woman said.

"May we come in for a minute please, Mrs Ward?" Burke said.

"Yes, if you must," she said standing aside to allow them to enter, "but what's all this about?"

Burke and Moore went into the hallway, and Mrs Ward directed them to the rear where a massive kitchen-diner was laid out all across the back of the property with picture windows looking out onto a paved patio and more of that immaculately maintained lawn.

"Sit down, for heaven's sake. I suppose you'd like a cup of tea?" Sheila Ward said.

"No thanks," Burke said, replying for both of them, "perhaps you'd like to take a seat yourself. I'm afraid we have some rather bad news."

Sheila Ward pulled out one of the kitchen chairs and sat down slowly, now looking much more worried.

Burke nodded to Moore.

"I'm afraid your sister, Brenda isn't it, was involved in a car accident a short time ago on the back road between Portmarnock and Malahide," Moore said.

"Accident? Are you sure? Brenda knows that road very well. She uses it every day. Did another car hit her?"

"We're not sure of the exact circumstances of the collision just yet, but it doesn't look as if there was any other vehicle involved, although we'll know more when our people have finished examining the scene," Moore said.

"Is she all right? Has she been taken to hospital?"

"I'm afraid it was a bit more serious than that, Sheila. I'm sorry to say Mrs Farrelly didn't survive the accident."

Sheila Ward stared blankly at Fiona Moore for what seemed like an eternity.

"No, no, she can't be gone. There's some kind of mistake. Maybe someone stole her car or something. Not after Jim, this is just too much!" Then the tears stated to flow.

Burke got up and pulled a few sheets of white kitchen paper off the roll that was standing on the kitchen worktop and handed it to the woman.

"Is there anyone here in the house with you, Sheila? What about your husband?"

Sheila Ward shook her head, and tried to compose herself.

"He's not here. He took off about a year ago with his secretary. They're living in some ghastly block of flats in Rathgar or somewhere. I don't see him anymore."

Burke and Moore exchanged glances.

"Is there anyone we can get to come and be with you, Sheila? It's a terrible shock for you," Moore said.

The woman shook her head again.

"No, there's no one. We didn't have any children. That's why Peter left me, or so he said, but I think he just wanted a younger model," she said bitterly.

Moore looked at Burke, who nodded almost imperceptibly.

"Well, I'll stay for a while, just till you get over the initial shock, Sheila. Is there a drop of brandy in the house?" Moore said.

"Yes, in the front room in the sideboard. Thanks."

Moore got up and went into the front room where a large antique mahogany sideboard stood along one wall. Burke had followed her into the room.

"Are you OK with this, Fiona?"

"Yes, of course. I'll sit with her a while and then try and get her to bed. You take my car, and I'll get a taxi back to town. Are you OK to drive?"

"Yes, I'm fine. Thanks. I'll leave it at the station and give the keys to the night man."

"Right. See you in the morning then."

Fiona Moore found a bottle of Courvoisier and a Waterford Crystal brandy glass and took both back into the kitchen. She poured a stiff measure and handed it to Sheila Ward.

"Have some yourself. I hardly ever touch the stuff."

"I'm OK, thanks. But is it OK if I make a cup of tea?"

"Yes, yes of course. Here, I'll do it," the woman said.

"No. You sit there and get that down you. I'll make us both a brew."

* * *

Fiona Moore and Sheila Ward stayed up for another two hours. Sheila had some more brandy, and seemed to be settling down a bit, although she did have a lot more questions for the detective about the car crash, most of which Moore couldn't answer.

"Can I see her?" Sheila said.

"Yes, of course. Tomorrow maybe. We need someone to identify the body in any case, but there's no doubt as to who it is. It's just a formality. I'll get someone out to collect you at, say, ten-thirty. Would that be OK?"

"Yes, thanks."

Moore accompanied the woman upstairs and saw her into bed before calling a local taxi firm and booking her ride back to the city centre. She wondered what further tragedy could possibly befall this unfortunate family, and why, if at all, they deserved such horrors.

Chapter Thirteen

When Burke arrived into work the following morning, Fiona Moore was already at her desk.

"Hi, boss. Did all that go OK last night?"

"Sure. What about you?"

Moore told him about spending time with Sheila Ward the previous evening.

"Must have been a late one," Burke said.

"Yeah, it was after two when I got my head down."

"OK, well we best get busy. See if we can get any further with Mr Farrelly's death. At least his wife's demise seems to have been an accident."

Moore looked at her boss, but didn't say anything.

"What? You don't think so?" Burke said.

"Well, I wouldn't put next month's salary on it. Not yet in any case. I've retrieved the dashcam memory card and I've sent her phone over to forensics to see what they can get off it. Let's see what they have to report – you heard her sister say she used that road every day."

"Yes, I know, but it was a powerful car. She probably just misjudged the corner. Let's not go looking for trouble if we don't have to. I was supposed to get a call back from

Farrelly's London office yesterday, but they never rang. I'm going to shake them up a bit. Want to listen in?"

"I wouldn't miss it for the world!" she said, getting up and following him into his office.

* * *

"Mr Wagstaff, this is Inspector Aidan Burke from the Irish police. I was hoping to speak to you yesterday about the unfortunate death of your colleague Jim Farrelly," Burke said, keen to drive home the fact that Wagstaff hadn't returned his call.

"Oh, yes, Inspector, very tragic. We are very busy here making alternative arrangements for Jim's clients. Unfortunately, things have to keep moving regardless."

"Ah yes, Mr Farrelly's clients. That's what I was hoping you could tell me. Who exactly were Mr Farrelly's clients?"

"I'd prefer if you got that information from our head office in Dublin, Inspector," Wagstaff said.

"And I'd prefer if you just told me, Mr Wagstaff. I don't want to have to bother the Metropolitan Police, although they could get a warrant and come round and find out for me if that's the way you want to do it," Burke said, looking at Moore who was enjoying the exchange.

Wagstaff remained silent for several moments, before admitting defeat.

"Well, you know he was working on this AMRAAL account, I'm sure. Then he was working on a patent application for an inventor who thinks he can reduce harmful emissions from motor vehicles by about seventy percent. And he was helping one of my colleagues here with a taxation case. A developer is being sued by the Inland Revenue for a large amount of tax, and they have been trying to minimize the liability, all perfectly legally of course."

"Is that the extent of it?" Burke asked.

"I think he was assisting with some smaller matters too. A few company formations and a merger we are looking after for a small chain of independent bookshops here. That's about it."

"Thank you. I wonder if I could trouble you to send me the full list with the names of the client companies and contact details by email?" Burke said, now that he had Wagstaff in a more compliant mood.

"Well, it's a bit irregular, but under the circumstances, I suppose so. But I'd prefer to route the email via Mr Mitchell in our Dublin office, if it's all the same to you, Inspector."

"Very well. Just as long as I have the information by close of business today. OK?"

Wagstaff agreed, albeit a little reluctantly, and the call was concluded.

"Nice one, boss. Could you really get the Met to go on a raid to their offices?" Moore said.

"I very much doubt it, but it appears to have worked."

Moore said nothing, but smiled.

"Right. Can you get onto the lab and see if they have anything back on Farrelly's toxicology yet? And chase up progress on his laptop as well. This is all taking too long for my liking."

Moore had seen Burke in this frame of mind many times in the past, and she knew better than to challenge him. She got up and left the room, wondering quite where to start.

* * *

Back in the general office, Moore asked Dónal Lawler to follow up on Farrelly's laptop while she contacted Daniel in forensics about the dead man.

"Hi, Daniel. The inspector is wondering if you have anything back on Jim Farrelly yet?"

"Well you will have seen the tox report – nasty business."

"Yes, someone knew what they were doing. Looks like quite a sophisticated operation," Moore said.

"It sure does. Certainly not an amateur job, that's for sure."

"By the way, who's working on his laptop?" Moore said.

"That's me. I'll have the replacement BIOS chip here a bit later, and then I'll have to do some work on the motherboard inside the machine. I'm hoping to have it opened up later today. Is that OK?"

"Yes, of course, it's just Inspector Burke is getting restless," Moore said.

"I'm working as fast as I can, Fiona. We're flat out here at the moment. He'll just have to cool it a bit," Daniel said defensively.

"Yes, I know, Daniel. I'm sorry, but you know what he's like. Let us know as soon as you have anything, won't you?"

"Sure, no problem. Now I really have to get back to it. Bye."

Moore sat back and contemplated her next move. She turned her attention to the internet, and started to dig up as much as she could on AMRAAL.

The first thing she learned was that the company had come about as a result of a union between two smaller pharmaceutical companies – Medical Licensing Inc. and American Analysis and Research Inc., which accounted for its current, rather unwieldy name. The two organisations had merged some three years ago. American Analysis and Research were the developers of Trebutivan, a process that had taken over ten years, during which time the company's fortunes had waxed and waned. In the latter stages of their solo existence, they had used Medical Licensing Inc. to help them to get through the labyrinth of processes associated with certification of the drug, and the licensing company realized that AAR was running out of cash, and could easily go broke before the drug was approved. Raising money for speculative pharmaceutical ventures was both difficult and very expensive. Following quite brief negotiations, the merger was agreed with MLI providing a healthy injection of money to allow the process of approval to be completed and, as they say, the rest is history. Trebutivan had been very successful in the market, and AMRAAL was now in a very healthy financial position largely on the back of the patent.

Then Moore turned her attention to the drug itself, which, unsurprisingly, she had never heard of. Initially, it seemed like a miracle cure for certain forms of kidney disease, which, up to the introduction of the product had been largely untreatable, resulting in dialysis or transplants for the afflicted. But as she began to dig further into the very many articles relating to the medicine, she started to come across papers describing adverse side effects. There weren't many, but those that there were spoke of very serious issues for a small number of patients taking the drug, leading inevitably to death. Many of the medical papers on the subject had come from East Asian countries such as South Korea and Japan, and they were quite scathing in their appraisal of the product. Moore searched around a bit more, but found almost no adverse publicity about Trebutivan in any Western publications. But she did find a rebuttal statement from AMRAAL about the negative publicity coming out of Japan. It simply said that the wonder drug had been administered to thousands of patients whose lives had been spared as a result, and that all medication has side effects, particularly where the patient has some underlying and possibly undetected medical condition. It was a clever piece of work. It didn't set out to deny the issue but rather to explain it, which ensured that AMRAAL could not be sued for false promotion. Moore wondered if this could in any way be connected to Jim Farrelly's unfortunate demise.

Chapter Fourteen

It was a cool autumn evening when Burke pulled his car up at the set-down area in front of the airport. Andrea had said that she would be on the last flight in from Gatwick, and as soon as Burke was inside the terminal building, he saw that the plane had landed ten minutes early.

Andrea had told him that she would work the first two Gatwick–Dublin–Gatwick flights as usual that Friday, but would swap the last flight so that she could travel as a passenger and remain in Dublin for the weekend.

Despite the flight's early landing, it seemed to take an age for the passengers to come out into the arrivals area, but eventually Andrea appeared, towing the regulation black wheelie-case behind her. She was dressed casually, with snug-fitting dark blue jeans – the expensive kind – a white shirt and a tan leather jacket. Her hair was loose around her shoulders and, as she approached, Burke thought that she looked terrific. There was a slightly awkward moment when they actually met, but Burke quickly took charge and leaned in and kissed her cheek.

"Hi, Andrea, you look great," he said. "Did you have a good flight?" he asked, taking her bag from her.

"Full flight. I had to travel in the jump seat on the flight deck, much to the delight of Karl and Marek who spent the entire fifty minutes ribbing me about my proposed weekend activities. Anyway, I'll get them back, don't worry."

"Do you get much aggravation as a female pilot? You know, sexism from the guys, that sort of thing."

"They try, but I give as good as I get, don't worry. And secretly I think they mostly admire the women. There are a good few of us now and we make quite good pilots, even if I say so myself. Sometimes there are even two females in charge of the aircraft, and the stewards tell us the passengers are quite surprised."

"I'm sure they are. I've never thought too much about the gender of whoever is in charge of the flight. Maybe it's because there are loads of good female police officers these days, though it wasn't like that when I first joined up."

"How long have you been in the police?"

"Gosh, I lose count. Let me see – I joined as a uniformed Garda, it must be almost twenty years ago, but I've been a detective for the last ten years."

"Wow. You must have seen some stuff," Andrea said.

"I guess. Anyway, here's my car."

"It's well for some. Priority parking, eh?"

"There has to be some advantages to being a cop!"

* * *

As they were leaving the airport complex, Burke said, "Are you hungry, Andrea? Did you get a chance to get a meal?"

"No, I didn't. I only just had time to change at the airport before the flight was called, and they absolutely hate it if crew are running late."

"Oh, OK. Well let's see if we can fix that to begin with. I think we might just be able to get a table at Rutlands. Could you handle a steak?"

"That would be wonderful. I hear the food in Dublin is supposed to be excellent. Are you hungry too?"

"Yes. I came straight from the office to the airport. We're having a busy time of it just now trying to solve Farrelly's murder."

"Is that the man who died on the flight?" Andrea said.

"Yes, the same. But it looks as if he was actually murdered with a very nasty kind of poison, and we need to find out where it was administered and of course by whom. Anyway, I'm off duty now. I've even turned my phone off for the weekend, so no more shop talk, OK?"

"Yes. You can be on holiday, like me," she said, and squeezed his hand.

* * *

Rutlands was a very busy steak house on the edge of Temple Bar in the city centre. It was always jammed, but Burke knew the man who owned it, which meant he was rarely turned away.

True to form, when they arrived, Burke caught the eye of the proprietor, and as if by magic, a table for two at the back of the restaurant became vacant.

"You're punching a bit above your weight tonight, Aidan," the man said as he showed them to their place, out of earshot of Andrea.

Burke just looked at him and smiled.

They were served quickly, and ate well. Andrea confirmed that the meal bore out the reputation of Dublin's food, and she put away a nice medium rare strip loin and salad with consummate ease.

Throughout the meal, they chatted casually about their own lives. Andrea was one of three girls born to a merchant in Sweden who dealt in agricultural imports and exports. Her sisters were both teachers, and she too would have followed that profession were it not for a slightly rebellious streak. At the age of sixteen she had won a competition for a day of flying at the local aero club, and ever since that she had been completely hooked. She had served her apprenticeship with SAS, but after a few years she left to join European Airways as they had a bigger route network and more opportunities for promotion.

Burke was quite happy to let her prattle on about herself. He enjoyed her accent, and liked hearing about her background which was so unlike his own.

At the end of the meal, Burke insisted on paying the bill, which Andrea initially resisted.

"You can get me back when I'm in Sweden," he said with a glint in his eye.

They drove out to Crumlin, where Burke's house was located. He had made a special effort to have the place spick and span for his visitor, with new, fresh bedlinen on her bed, and fluffy white towels piled up with a facecloth, soap and even a toothbrush still in its wrapper and a small tube of Colgate all awaiting her arrival.

He took her case up to the room with Andrea following, and placed it on the floor by the window.

"Here we are," he said with a flourish. "I'm afraid there's no en-suite, but the bathroom is just across the landing. It's nice and quiet here at the back of the house. You should sleep well."

They went back downstairs, and Burke offered his guest a whiskey or a brandy as a nightcap, but Andrea declined.

"No thanks, Aidan. But maybe if you have a small glass of white wine?"

"Yes, of course."

Burke went and got the drinks for them both, and they settled down on the sofa beside each other.

The conversation was easy, and as the clock went around into the early morning, Burke felt that they could have chatted all night long. But when Andrea stifled a yawn, he realized she had done a long day's work, and was probably quite tired.

"I think it's time for bed, Andrea. You go on. I'll just tidy up a bit here. What time do you like to get up?"

"Anytime is fine by me. What about nine or nine-thirty?"

"Yes, that's very civilized. See you then."

* * *

Burke had prepared quite a spread for breakfast. Knowing the Swedish penchant for cold meats and cheeses along with bread rolls and jam, he had laid out an array of same on the dresser in the kitchen and had a nice big pot of strong, freshly ground coffee on the go when Andrea appeared just after nine-twenty.

"Good morning, Andrea. Did you sleep OK?"

"Yes, I slept very soundly, thank you. You have been to a lot of trouble for me, Aidan. I'm not used to being pampered." She sidled over to him, put her arms around his middle and gave him a toothpasty kiss.

When they had breakfasted, Burke asked Andrea what she would like to do for the day.

"I'd like to see some of the sights. Maybe Trinity College and the Art Gallery. Are they close together?"

"Yes, very. That would be an easy one. And if you like we could have a look at the State Apartments too. They are quite impressive. They form part of Dublin Castle which was the seat of the Viceroy of Ireland up until 1922. Before that, Ireland was ruled by the British. It was the main administrative centre for the government, and now houses various Irish government offices."

"Sounds good. I've brought my camera too. Are we allowed to take photographs?"

"Yes, of course, in fact it's almost compulsory."

* * *

By mid-afternoon the two of them were getting tired. After visiting Dublin Castle, they had walked up along Dame Street to Trinity College. The queue for the Book of

Kells was too long to endure, but they walked all around the campus, and Andrea expressed surprise that such a large area could be devoted to a university right in the middle of the city.

"It's been here since 1592," Burke said. "Its official title is the College of the Holy and Undivided Trinity of Queen Elizabeth – that's Queen Elizabeth the first by the way – but that's quite a mouthful, so everybody calls it Trinity College these days."

"Wow! 1592. So it's over four hundred years old. Did you go to college here, Aidan?"

"Not a chance. I attended UCD. That's the other big college in Dublin. There is great rivalry between them, but this place is considered more prestigious due to its age and provenance. It was originally modelled on Oxford University in England."

"Cool. It certainly has atmosphere, and some very beautiful buildings."

The couple then went out the back gate of Trinity onto Lincoln Place, and strolled around to Merrion Square before going into the National Gallery where they spent over two hours browsing. Andrea was very impressed with the collections of old masters that were on display. They had grabbed a light lunch in the restaurant in the gallery, but by three-thirty, they were both fading a little.

"What would you like to do now, Andrea? Would you like to see some of the shops in Grafton Street? It's the best shopping street in the city, and it's quite close."

Andrea took his hand, and said in a low voice, "Funny business."

Burke looked at her with a puzzled expression.

She leaned in closer to him and took his other hand in hers too.

"When you invited me to stay, you said there would be no funny business. But sometimes that's just what a girl needs." She planted a soft, gentle kiss on his lips.

Burke put his arm around her as they walked back to his parked car.

Chapter Fifteen

Fiona Moore arrived at Store Street Garda station at close to ten o'clock on that Saturday. She had decided that there was too much going on to leave things till Monday, and in any case, some of the reports from forensics might be in by now, and she was keen to see what they contained. She wasn't disappointed.

The first piece of news was from Daniel. An email, saying simply, 'call me when you get this'. Moore lifted the phone, but didn't think that he would be available at the weekend, and was surprised when he answered.

"Hi, Daniel, it's Fiona. You were looking for me."

"Yes, hi, Fiona. Can I ask where you are?"

"I'm at the station, why?"

"Great. Can I pop over?"

"Sure, and bring some doughnuts or muffins or something and some coffee. I'll pay you when you get here."

"Great. See you soon."

While Moore waited for Daniel and sustenance to arrive, she went looking for the post-mortem report on Brenda Farrelly. It had been uploaded to their computer system, and she read it with interest.

Mrs Farrelly had been in generally very good health. She was of average weight for her height, and her major organs all seemed to be functioning as expected. But as Moore read on, she came to a surprising fact. Brenda Farrelly's tox report showed that she had ingested large quantities of a sedative shortly before her death. The substance was lorazepam, and Moore had to check, but she was certain that it was the same product that the woman's husband had been dosed with before he passed away.

"Well, that could explain her erratic driving, I suppose," Moore said to herself, but she decided to wait for Daniel to arrive before investigating further. She didn't have long to wait.

The young man arrived accompanied by his laptop, and balancing a cardboard tray containing two takeaway coffee cups, with a paper bag suspended awkwardly underneath.

"Here, let me give you a hand," Moore said, getting up to relieve Daniel of his burden.

They tucked into the coffee and the delicious pastries, and when they had eaten, Moore said, "So, Daniel, what brings you into work on the weekend with all this mystery?"

"Mystery is right. You're not going to believe this," he said, gesturing towards his computer. He opened it, and brought up an image of a small, square, black item set alongside a ruler which indicated that the object was roughly eight centimetres square with a black and a red wire protruding from inside.

"What's that?" Moore said.

"That, Sergeant, is a modification to the engine control unit on Mrs Farrelly's car. One of the lads going over the vehicle after the crash found it. It was wired into the cruise control mechanism, and it apparently caused the car to accelerate uncontrollably when certain conditions were encountered."

"Cripes! What conditions?"

"The lads are still working on it, but it looks like when she braked heavily after the car was warmed up, this thing cut in and caused the car to speed up, which is probably why she crashed into the bridge. She wouldn't have been able to stop the car, and in any case, you will have seen that she was probably very groggy from the sedative that was in her system."

"Blimey. Very thorough. So, we're looking at a second murder then?" Moore said.

"Yes, it looks like that."

"But why would anyone want to kill the wife? I mean, she wasn't involved with her husband's work as far as we can tell."

"That's for you to find out, Fiona. We just dig this stuff up."

"I'm going to call Aidan. This is a bit above my pay grade."

Moore dialled her colleague's mobile number, but it just went to voicemail advising the caller to call Store Street, and providing the number for the station.

"Damn. He's off the air. Have you anything else, Daniel?"

"Oh, yes, I nearly forgot. I've managed to get into Jim Farrelly's laptop. I had to resolder the motherboard with a new BIOS chip. But that worked, so I have access to the contents now. But I haven't had a chance to look at any of the stuff yet."

"Right, well can you concentrate on that for now? Focus on anything to do with this American pharma outfit, AMRAAL. Look for emails and any documents that look meaty. But keep it tight. This could be very sensitive. Sorry to hassle you, but is there anything of significance back from the aircraft Farrelly came in on?"

"We've sent the garbage, the remainder of the catering, and anything else we could remove from the plane, up to The Park and the team up there. I haven't heard anything back, but I'll follow it up as soon as I get a chance."

"Why don't I do that. You have your hands full already," Moore said.

"Would you? Thanks, that would be great. Give Máiréad Webster a call. She was looking after it."

When Daniel had returned to his natural habitat, Moore remembered the little card she had taken from the dashcam in Mrs Farrelly's car. She retrieved the item, and slipped it into the card reader on her computer. After a bit of fiddling about, she was able to get the VLC programme to play the footage which was conveniently sequenced in reverse order, so the latest footage came first. The latest sequence was nearly five minutes long, and showed Mrs Farrelly's car reversing out of their driveway, then going forward, out of the estate and onto the back road that connected Portmarnock to the coast.

The footage was uneventful for a couple of kilometres, but as Mrs Farrelly approached the bridge where the accident had taken place, the vehicle suddenly sped up. It was a powerful car, and by the time it hit the bridge it had achieved a speed of over 90kph which was much too fast to negotiate the bends in the road that corkscrewed around under the old stone railway bridge.

Moore watched, transfixed, as the vehicle went sideways and then slammed into the stonework before tilting up on its side and turning over. The dashcam kept recording faithfully until the car came to rest in a cloud of steam and smoke, and even captured the screams of the woman driving as she tried in vain to control the runaway vehicle.

The witness's account appeared to be correct. There was no sign of any other vehicle being involved in the crash, nor any rational explanation for the manner in which the car accelerated before it hit the bridge. The findings of the technical team concerning the modification to Mrs Farrelly's car must be correct, Moore reflected.

"Damn it! I wish Burke wasn't AWOL. This is turning into a right old puzzle," she said to herself, ejecting the memory card and placing it back carefully in a small evidence bag.

* * *

It was getting on for lunchtime when Moore got around to calling the forensic team up in The Park. She got through to Máiréad almost immediately.

"Hi, Máiréad, it's Detective Sergeant Fiona Moore here from Store Street. I believe you have been analysing the stuff that was taken off the European Airways plane the evening Jim Farrelly died."

"Oh, yes hello, Fiona, we've been through all the left-over food, the rubbish that was collected, and the flight attendants' personal belongings were searched on the night too. I'm afraid there's nothing. There was a slight trace of the poison on the armrest of his seat, but that almost certainly came from him rubbing his face. If I was to bet on it, I'd say he ingested the stuff long before he got on the flight. Sorry I can't be more helpful."

"Not at all. In a funny way, you may have been very helpful. Tox have told us the stuff was in his system for some time in any case, judging by the effect on his internal organs, so it looks as if he got it either sometime during his away day, or maybe even before he left Ireland. Thanks anyway. Have you completed your analysis?"

"Yes, we have. European Airways were busting to get their plane back, so we had to be quick," Máiréad said.

"I'll bet they were. OK, well thanks for the information. We'll talk again."

Chapter Sixteen

Fiona Moore spent the afternoon updating the Garda computer system with all the information that had come in about the car and the details of the substance found in Mrs Farrelly. She was very miffed that the SIO was still uncontactable, so by teatime she decided to head home.

"There's little point in me slaving away over nothing when Burke isn't here. Damn! I wonder what he is up to?" she said to herself, packing away her stuff and putting on her jacket.

Her journey home took her through Sandymount village, and as she rounded the bend leading onto the village green, she spotted Burke's car parked at the side of the road. She slowed right down, and did another circuit of the green to see if she could see any sign of her boss. As she drove past Ambrosia, a fashionable chic bistro with a large plate-glass window looking out onto the street, she saw Aidan Burke and Andrea Bergin seated near the front of the restaurant. They were clearly enjoying each other's company, and each had a tall glass of wine and a plate of what looked to be delicious food in front of them. They were chatting and laughing with each other like giddy teenagers.

"So, that's your game, is it, DI Burke? Just you wait till Monday. Gotcha!" she said to herself, smirking as she drove off towards home.

* * *

On Sunday, Aidan Burke and Andrea Bergin spent a lazy morning in bed. Andrea was due to fly back to Gatwick on the mid-afternoon service, so as lunchtime approached Burke said to her, "Why don't we get up, have some breakfast, and then I'll drive you to the airport via Malahide, maybe have a look at the old castle and gardens?"

"Sounds great. Is it far from the airport?"

"No. In fact you probably fly over it almost every time you come in to land at Dublin, or nearly over it in any case."

"If it's that close, we're usually concentrating on the landing, making sure our speed is OK and that we are centred on the glideslope for the final approach."

"Right, sounds like fun. Anyway, out you get. I'll cook breakfast. Scrambled eggs and bacon OK?"

"Mmm. Sounds perfect, and lots of strong coffee please!"

"Yes, ma'am!" he said, giving her a friendly pat on the rear.

* * *

After the late breakfast they drove out to the grounds of Malahide Castle.

As they strolled around the expansive parkland in front of the castle itself, Burke gave a potted history of the place to his companion.

"The castle dates from the twelfth century, and was owned by the same family, the Talbots, for nearly 800 years. It has an interesting history. During the First World War it was used as a base for British airships. It was finally sold to the state to settle death duties in 1975, and was later saved from the bulldozers by Charles Haughey who was our prime minister at the end of the seventies. Some say it's one of the most useful things he did for the country. As you can see it's a terrific amenity, and they use the castle itself from time to time for state banquets."

"Yes, it's huge, and I can see lots of sports facilities over there," Andrea said, pointing to the many football pitches marked out on the other side of the main driveway.

They walked around for another half an hour or so, and then Andrea said she had better make a move to get to the airport.

"I can't be late for the flight, Aidan, much as I'd like to stay a bit longer."

Burke squeezed her hand affectionately, and said, "There will be other times, Andrea, that is, if you want that?"

"I do," came the simple reply, and they put their arms around each other walking back to the car.

On the way to the airport, Burke asked if Andrea would have to travel back in the cockpit.

"No, not this time, thank heavens. The booked load is only 162, so there will be plenty of spare seats."

"That reminds me. On the day Jim Farrelly died, would it have been the same set of flight attendants that were working the early morning flight from Dublin to Gatwick?"

"Probably. That service originates in Gatwick. It leaves at just after six, and the return flight departs Dublin at five past eight, so it probably was the same crew OK. I know I flew the early sectors anyway," Andrea said.

"God, you must have to get up very early for that!"

"Tell me about it. My alarm goes off at three forty-five. I have to be in the airport by ten past five for the briefing on Fridays. During the week is easier."

They reached the airport and Burke parked directly outside the terminal, placing the Garda on Duty sign in the windscreen.

"You're funny, Aidan. Do you not get into trouble for doing that?"

"There have been no complaints so far."

Before Andrea disappeared through into the departure area, they kissed warmly.

"When will I see you?" Burke said as Andrea disengaged.

"Whenever you like," she said with an impish smile, and then she was gone.

* * *

When Burke got home, he reluctantly switched on his mobile phone. Unsurprisingly, there were several voicemails from Fiona Moore, the later ones sounding quite exasperated.

"Where the hell are you, boss? I need to talk to you. There have been some very significant developments. Call me as soon as you get this."

Burke thought for a moment, and then selected his colleague's number from his contact list and dialled.

"Hi, Fiona, it's me. You were looking for me. What's up?"

"Ah, so you are actually alive then. I've been trying to contact you."

"Yes, I know. I was busy. But I'm here now. Why all the fuss?"

"Look, I can't go into it all now on the phone. At this stage it will keep till morning. Will you be joining us, or you still on walkabout?"

"No, I'll be in bright and early at eight. Are you sure there's nothing I can do now?"

"No. It's OK. I'll see you at eight."

* * *

On the way back to Gatwick, Andrea Bergin reflected on the weekend that she had spent in Dublin in the company of Detective Inspector Aidan Burke. Was she right to get so close to this man? She was certainly attracted to him, and then some, but things were complicated enough without bringing a whole new dimension to the situation. But then she remembered their intimacy, and the natural warmth that she experienced in his arms and in his bed. It was something she wasn't used to, and she liked it – a lot.

"Ah, what the hell," she said to herself, staring out the window at the fluffy clouds and the patchwork of fields below. "Go with the flow, Andrea."

Chapter Seventeen

In Store Street the following morning, Burke was more relaxed than Moore had seen him in a long time. His humour was cheerful too. It was most unlike the usual 'Monday morning grouch' she was used to.

"Hi, Fiona. Like to come into my office and we can do a catch-up?" he said breezily.

Moore followed him in and sat down.

"OK, well I'm not sure how up to date you are with this case. But we now know that Mrs Farrelly appears to have been murdered along with her husband. Her car had been tampered with and she had been drugged to boot."

"Christ! So, we have two murders to solve. Anything else?"

"Yes. Daniel has been able to get into Farrelly's laptop. He'll be working on it today to see what it can tell us. And I did a bit of research on Farrelly's clients, AMRAAL. It seems there's some controversy about their big patent, Trebutivan, but they've managed to keep it more or less under wraps, except in Asia."

"Yes, but that's hardly likely to have involved Farrelly. I mean from what Kendron Mitchell told us, Farrelly was just doing some corporate work for them to do with setting up in Ireland."

"Yes, but what if he had discovered something really big about Trebutivan, and his curiosity took him to places that they'd rather he didn't go?" Moore said.

"Hmm, unlikely in my view. No. What this needs is some old-fashioned police work. Have you been onto Farrelly's doctor to see what medication he was taking regularly, if any?"

"No, not yet. It was the weekend, remember."

"And what about beneficiaries of his death, and the wife too? I believe they didn't have kids. See if you can track down a will at all. His firm probably have it. And we'd better look into his personal finances too. See if he has any big debts or any odd payments coming his way that don't look right. Same for the wife. Oh, and something else occurred to me over the weekend. I wonder if the same set of cabin attendants were on his flight out to Gatwick on the Friday. We still don't know when or where he got the poison, so it might be worth checking that out."

"Was Andrea Bergin not able to tell you that?"

Burke looked sternly at his junior officer and said nothing for a minute.

Moore stared back, until eventually Burke said, "How the hell did you know about that?"

"Well, I am a fucking detective, boss, or had you forgotten?" With that, she got up and left the room.

Back outside in the open plan, she tried to analyse her emotions. Was she just hacked off because she had been left on her own to deal with a difficult case for two days, or was there a hint of jealousy in her reaction to her boss's new love interest? After a few moments pondering the situation, she shrugged it off and got on with her work.

* * *

"Dr Leahy? My name is Detective Sergeant Fiona Moore from Store Street. We're investigating the sudden death of one of your patients, a Mr Jim Farrelly."

"Oh, yes, terrible business. I don't understand it. He was as fit as a flea last time I saw him. I understand he died of a heart attack on board a plane. Is that right?"

"When exactly did you last see him, Dr Leahy?"

"Let me see now. Yes, here it is. Just two months ago. He had to have a check-up every year for his company. They have a fairly sizeable death in service policy that pays out a big amount in the event of this kind of thing, and the insurance company insist."

"And was he in good shape when you saw him?" Moore said.

"Yes, very much so. Not a bit overweight. Blood pressure absolutely normal. ECG normal too. Jim was in excellent order all round, I'd say. That's why I don't understand how his heart gave up on him so suddenly."

"Was Mr Farrelly on any medication, Doctor?"

"Nothing much. He took 20mg of statins daily, and I know he was keen on a few vitamins and some dietary supplements, but of course I didn't prescribe those, I just gave him the statins."

"Is that normal, in your view?"

"Oh, yes. I recommend all my male patients over forty-five take a small amount of statins. Especially those with a somewhat sedentary lifestyle. But it was nothing out of the ordinary."

"And did you ever prescribe a tranquillizer for Mr Farrelly, specifically lorazepam?"

"Good heavens, no. What made you think of that?"

"Oh, nothing. It's not important. Thanks, Doctor. What about Mrs Farrelly? Was she a patient of yours too?"

"No, she had her own GP locally in Malahide, I believe."

"Right, well thanks for the information. If I need anything further, I'll be in touch."

"Very well. Goodbye, Sergeant."

When Moore had finished the call to the good doctor, she walked over to where Dónal Lawler was sitting.

"Hi, Dónal. Listen, I want you to start digging into Farrelly's finances. The boss wants all we can get on his personal money, and you'd better include the wife too. They looked to be quite well heeled, but you never know."

"OK, Sarge. Do we know where they banked?" Lawler asked.

"I think his bank card was in his wallet. It'll be in the evidence room along with his other stuff. That will get you started."

"Great, thanks."

As Moore walked back to her own desk, she had an idea. She called the pathologist.

"Hi, Aileen, it's Fiona. Listen, I was wondering if you have been able to pin down the time that Jim Farrelly was administered the ricin that killed him?"

"Hi, Fiona. Yes, I was going to call you. We've been doing a lot more work on his organs. This is a very unusual case for us, so the gang here are fascinated by it. Of course, we don't have much local knowledge to apply, but there's loads of stuff on the net and in various journals. I'm reasonably certain that the poison was administered to Farrelly on the day that he died, possibly quite early on that morning, certainly before midday."

"I see. Can you be any more precise?" Moore said.

"Not officially, but off the record, I'd wager sometime between six and ten in the morning. But don't quote me on that."

"OK, that's a big help actually. What about the missus. Can you tell when she got her dose of tranquillizers?"

"Yes, that's much easier. They were ingested two hours before the accident, give or take half an hour either way. Does that help?" Brophy said.

"Not really. I mean it's useful to know, but I'm damned if I can understand why the woman would take that amount of Ativan in the middle of the afternoon."

"Sorry. Can't help with that, I'm afraid. Over to you now."

"Yes, I know. Thanks, Aileen. Send all that over in a report, will you?"

"Yes, of course."

While Dónal Lawler was exploring the Farrelly finances, Moore decided that she would contact Sheila Ward, Mrs Farrelly's sister. She made the call, and arranged to drive out to see the woman in half an hour. She elected to wait until she returned to tell her boss the newly discovered information. Before she left, she collected Amy Sutton and told her what they were up to.

Chapter Eighteen

Moore and Sutton drove out to Sheila Ward's house in Kinsealy. Sutton observed that the house was being slowly surrounded by new development, and was one of the few spacious residences that had, so far, been more or less untouched by the advancing housing estates. She reckoned that the property, which appeared to be on a decent-sized plot, would be worth a good few euro when it eventually succumbed to the bulldozers. They got out of the car and approached the front door. Moore rang the bell, and turned around to admire the garden, as she wondered what the Wards occupied themselves with to keep them in such prosperity. A moment later, the door opened and Sheila Ward welcomed Fiona Moore.

Sheila Ward bore a close resemblance to her dead sister. They were both blonde, and stood at about 170cm, although Moore guessed that Sheila was the elder, but not by much.

"Come in, please. Can I get you a cup of tea or coffee, ladies?"

"No thanks," Moore said, answering for both of them.

"Oh, OK. Just come through here then, and we can have a chat. What's on your mind?" she said as she led the way into the nicely furnished front lounge that overlooked the garden. She gestured for the two detectives to sit down.

"I'm sorry to bother you at this time, Mrs Ward, but we need to try and find out all we can about your sister and brother-in-law. Needless to say, it's most unusual for a married couple to pass on the same week in these circumstances."

"Yes, of course. I understand, but to be honest, the whole thing is still very raw. Have you found out any more about my sister's accident?"

Moore and Sutton exchanged a swift glance before Amy Sutton spoke up.

"I'm sorry to have to tell you, Mrs Ward, but I'm afraid it wasn't quite an accident."

The woman frowned and said, "How do you mean? Her car hit the bridge. Was there another vehicle involved that I don't know about?"

"No, nothing like that. As is routine in these cases, our forensics team went over the car very thoroughly, and I'm sorry to say, it had been tampered with. The cruise control mechanism had been modified which is why Mrs Farrelly's car sped up just at that point in the road."

"Oh, my God, I had no idea," Sheila Ward said, putting her hand to her face in horror.

"So, naturally, we need to investigate both of their lives thoroughly. I'm sure you understand," Moore said.

"May I ask if your sister was on any tranquillizers or sedatives, Mrs Ward?" Moore said.

"No. At least I don't think so. No, she would have told me, I'm sure. Why?"

"It's just that there was quite an amount of tranquillizer found in her blood. Probably enough to make driving tricky."

"That's ridiculous!"

"I know this is hard, Mrs Ward, but can you tell us if Brenda had been depressed before her husband died?" Sutton asked.

"No. Far from it. She wasn't that way inclined at all. She always had a very positive attitude."

"What about their relationship. Were they happy together?"

"Yes, very. At least as far as I know. You never really know what goes on behind closed doors, but they seemed to be very content."

"Was she OK with them having no children?" Moore asked.

"Yes. We talked about that from time to time. Neither of us have kids, and that's deliberate, before you ask."

Amy Sutton decided to change direction as they didn't seem to be getting anywhere.

"What does your husband do, Mrs Ward?"

"Anyone he can get his hands on! No wait, that's not fair. But he left me for a younger model four years ago. They're shacked up somewhere on the south side. I haven't seen him for ages which suits me just fine."

"And do you work, Mrs Ward?" Moore asked.

"No. I don't have to. Our parents were quite wealthy and they left a sizeable trust fund for both of us when they passed on. And then Peter pays a generous allowance as well. This place is owned outright, and at least he had the decency to sign it over before he went off with your one."

"What is it that he works at, Mr Ward, I mean?" Sutton asked.

"He's in electronics. He has a factory on the Naas Road and they make stuff for Intel and IBM, I think. He does very well. At least that's what he told me a while back. It may not be the same now."

"Did Mr Ward have much to do with your sister and Jim when he was still here, Mrs Ward?" Moore said.

"Not especially. We'd have dinner together for birthdays and things, and we usually went to one or the other's house at Christmas if we were all in the country, but that was about it. Why do you ask?"

"As I said, Mrs Ward, we're just trying to build a picture for now. This is a very unusual case. I'm sorry to have to ask this, but as far as you are aware, were Jim and Brenda faithful to each other?"

"Yes, yes I'm sure they were. Brenda and I were quite close. We spoke to each other every day, and she never gave the slightest hint that there was anything amiss between them. I think I would have known if she was spoofing. They seemed devoted, to be honest. I have to say, there were times when I felt quite envious of her. She seemed to have it all."

"Right, well, thanks very much for seeing us, Mrs Ward. We'll leave you in peace, and once again, I'm sorry if we had to ask some difficult questions. If you think of anything else that might be of any help with any of this, please give me a call," Moore said, handing the woman a business card.

As they drove back to town, Moore asked Amy Sutton what she thought of the interview.

"I dunno. She seemed honest enough. Do you think she was covering anything up, Sarge?"

"Not sure. If she was, she was damned good at it. Did you spot anything at all?"

"Well, just that her estranged hubby is into electronics, and Brenda Ward's car had an electronic modification, but that's probably just a coincidence," Sutton said.

"Hmm… maybe," Moore said. She didn't really believe in coincidences.

Chapter Nineteen

Back at Store Street Garda station, information was accumulating thick and fast. There were the transcripts from Jim Farrelly's laptop that contained various minutes, agendas and contemporaneous notes that he had made at meetings, and his entire diary for the year was detailed as well. Financial data on the Farrellys had come in from the banks, and the techies had managed to gain access to both of the phones Farrelly had on him on the day he died, and all the details of their contents was documented as well.

When Moore saw the pile of stuff that was apparently demanding her immediate attention, she felt completely overwhelmed. She went in search of her boss.

Burke was in his office mulling over some of the information that had come in.

"Hi, Fiona. What's up?"

"Look, boss, there's about half a ton of stuff outside that all needs to be gone through. Plus we need to get records for Farrelly from European Airways, and I haven't completed the trawl through the stuff from his office yet either. We need help."

"Yeah, I know, and that's not all either," Burke said.

"What do you mean?"

"I think we need to interview the cabin attendants from Farrelly's flight again. I've read over the pathologist's report, and she says he could have been given the ricin on the morning of his flight between six and ten. Well, for at least an hour of that four-hour window, he was a guest of European Airways. Maybe he was given it on the flight."

"Christ, boss, are you serious?"

"Never more so. So, let's get everyone together for a few minutes now and divvy up the tasks. Then we'll see about how we can get in front of Marta and her crew as soon as possible."

"Yes, and we mustn't forget the flight crew too – who was it, Kaan and Bergin."

"I don't see how they could have had anything to do with it," Burke said defensively.

"Don't you? Listen, boss, are you sure whatever is going on between you and the pilot lady is entirely appropriate given the circumstances? I'd hate to see you compromised in any way."

"That's none of your business, Fiona. Just leave it. OK?"

"Yes, boss, I hear you." But she was very uneasy, and again she wondered if the green-eyed monster was not at work in some way, but she quickly dismissed the notion.

* * *

Dónal Lawler, Amy Sutton and Daniel from forensics were all seated in the open plan when Burke and Moore came in.

Burke addressed the little group.

"Right, guys. There is a barrowload of information that's come in about Jim Farrelly and his wife, and we need to sift through it quickly to see if there are any clues as to how or why they were both murdered. Is everyone OK for a bit of overtime on this one?"

"Yes, sir," they all said in unison.

"Good. Well, here's what I want. Amy, can you take the financial information that we have on the couple. Go back about six months and look for anything unusual going in or out of their accounts. Summarize it on a page or less, or make up a small spreadsheet or whatever. I don't want to know how much they spent on cat food, but anything that strikes you as unusual. You get the picture?"

"Yes, sir. I understand."

"Good. Now, Dónal, I want you to work with Daniel on the tech stuff. We need to know where the device installed in Mrs Farrelly's car was made and preferably by whom. And find out if the car had been serviced or in a garage recently. Then look at her dashcam footage and see if you can trace her movements over the last few days. Anything at all may help us. Have we got the details from Farrelly's phones yet?" Burke said looking at Daniel.

"No, sir, not yet. But there is something a bit odd."

"What's that?"

"Well, the little Nokia he had in his pocket has been used just to call one single number. The trace goes back a few months, and there are text messages and calls on it. I haven't analysed them yet, but it strikes me as a bit odd if that was his personal phone, if you see what I mean."

"Do we know who the other phone – the one he was calling and texting – belongs to?"

"No, sir, not yet. They were both unregistered."

"Right. Well, stay on it. We need to find out what was going on there. Can you give me the number that he was calling from it, Daniel?"

Daniel turned to the nearest desk and took a scrap of paper on which he wrote the number, handing it to Burke.

"Now, lastly, Fiona. I'd like you to concentrate on European Airways. We need to get a list of the flights that Farrelly took over the last, say, three months, and compare them to his diary and whatever the assistant girl, what was her name, Miriam, yes that's it, has in her records," Burke said.

"Do you mean you want to confirm that he was where he said he was? That sort of thing?"

"Exactly!"

"And what are you going to do, boss?" Moore asked.

"I'm going to see if we can track down the flight attendants and get to talk to them. And I want it face to face, so we may have to go to the UK or wherever they are based this week."

"OK, boss. Right, everyone. Let's meet up again at six o'clock and see what we have all found out."

* * *

Moore could hear her boss slowly losing his temper in his office, culminating with him slamming the phone down loudly and cursing out loud. She went in to see what was going on.

"Hey, what's up?"

"Fucking European Airways, that's what's up. I can't get to speak to a human. It's all press 2 for this, 3 for that and eventually it just goes around in a circle back to where you started from. It's driving me mad!"

"Hang on. I might be able to help," Moore said. She took out her pocketbook and leaned over Burke's desk to access his phone and dialled a number.

"Hello, is that Rory? Rory Dillon?" Moore asked.

"Yes, who's this?" said the voice at the other end of the line.

"It's Detective Sergeant Moore. We met out at the airport the night that guy died on the Gatwick flight – remember?"

"Jesus! I'll never forget it. How can I help, Sergeant?"

"I was wondering if you could give me a direct phone number for your cabin crew management people? We need to get in touch with the cabin attendants that were on that flight."

"Sure. Hold on a sec."

Moore waited listening to the sound of paper being thumbed.

"Yeah, here we go. If you call 805 7878 you'll get straight through to them. Ask for a Joe Byrne or Mary Looney. They are in charge there."

"Thanks a million, Rory, that's great. Bye."

Moore turned to Burke and said, "Now, there you go, boss. Do you want to call them, or will I?"

Burke took the number from Moore with an ungrateful glare, and dialled the number. He got speaking to Joe Byrne immediately and told him what they needed.

"You're in luck, Inspector. Firstly, they are all still together. They're doing a Zagreb to Dublin flight tomorrow night. It gets in here around eight-thirty. How long do you need them for?" Byrne asked.

"We could probably use about two hours with them. Can that be arranged?"

"I guess so. I'll juggle a few things here and put them on the late flight to Stansted. That leaves at eleven-twenty, so you'll have two and a half hours clear, and anyway that Zagreb flight is nearly always early."

"Thanks, Joe. That's more than helpful. But just one more thing. Don't let them know we want to interview them please. Just tell them it's an operational change. OK?"

"Yes, sure, no problem. I won't be on duty when you get here tomorrow, but Rory should be around. Ask anyone for him and he'll set you up in a room somewhere."

When the call was over, Burke said to Moore, "Thanks, Fiona. Sorry if I snapped at you. This thing is doing my head in."

"You're grand, boss. Glad to help."

Chapter Twenty

Burke brought everyone together for a meeting as the day wore on.

"Right, everyone, we have a lot of new information now, so we need to set up some actions."

He went on to explain about the burner phone that had been found in Jim Farrelly's pocket, and the interview he had arranged with the European Airways cabin crew for the following evening.

"I want to interview the flight attendants individually, so all four of us will go to the airport tomorrow evening and take a careful note of what they say so that we can compare notes afterwards. In the meantime, can we start background checks on all of them?"

"What are we looking for, boss?" Dónal Lawler asked.

"Any previous form that any of them may have, no matter how trivial. Known associates, if we can get that far, and if you can, Dónal, details of their bank accounts, although that could be tricky. But if all else fails, we can ask them during the interview. Being largely Eastern European, they may not be aware of the limitations we work under here," Burke said.

"Do you not think that's a bit dodgy, boss?" Fiona Moore said.

"So is murder, Sergeant, and remember we have two of them now."

Moore said nothing, but had a slightly uneasy feeling about her boss's plan.

"Now, I want all of us to put the number that Farrelly was calling in secret into your own phones. Then I want you, Fiona, to go back to Mrs Ward's place on some pretext, and when you are there, call that number discreetly and see if you can hear anything ringing. I know these methods are a little unconventional, but we're up against it, and the man above is getting very impatient."

"What are you going to do, boss?" Moore asked.

"I'm going back to Milligan Walker. I want to try the phone trick out in the presence of that Miriam. She looks to be like a possible candidate for Farrelly's affections. She's not unattractive, and having an affair with your secretary has been known."

A murmur went through the group.

"What would you like me to do, sir?" Amy Sutton asked.

"Yes, Amy, I'm just coming to that. I'm afraid I need you to work on Farrelly's laptop. I want you to explore his email account or accounts, and see if you can find anything at all that might give us a clue as to why he was taken out. Look for any derogatory emails about any of his clients, or any of their practices, and pull anything that looks interesting and print it off. We'll look at them later if there is anything. OK?"

"Yes, sir. Oh, and may I ask a question, sir?"

"Of course, Amy," Burke said.

"What about the flight crew, Piotr Kaan and Andrea Bergin? Are we going to interview them again too?" Sutton asked innocently. She didn't know about Burke's connection to the blonde Swedish co-pilot.

Moore squirmed uneasily in her seat.

"I don't think that's necessary, Amy. They told us that they don't interact with the passengers except via the intercom to make announcements, and the flight deck door is locked all the time anyway. It would have been very peculiar if either of them had come back into the cabin on a 50-minute flight. But make a note to ask the cabin staff if anything like that took place, just to be certain," Burke said.

Moore couldn't resist interjecting.

"Shouldn't we include them in our background checks though, just for completeness?" she said.

Burke gave her a hard stare.

"No, Fiona. Just leave it, will you? We have enough to be doing without chasing our tails."

"Very well, sir, whatever you say," she said with a slight smirk.

"Oh, and speaking of completeness, there is one other avenue we need to check out, even though I suspect it will be pointless. Sheila Ward told us that her ex-husband is into electronics. He has a factory in Naas, it seems, that makes components for IBM and Intel. Can someone just do a background check on him too? Just the usual stuff."

"I'll sort that, boss," Lawler said obligingly.

"Thanks, Dónal. Right, let's get to it. Call me if anything useful pops up, and we'll meet again tomorrow morning to talk about the interviews out at the airport later. Oh, and I nearly forgot. Has anyone got the records from European Airways of Farrelly's trips for the last three months?"

There was no reply from anyone.

"OK. Well, Amy, could I ask you to follow that up for us too. It could be important."

* * *

Burke arrived at the offices of Milligan Walker soon after four o'clock. It seemed that the place was emptying out, which struck him as odd, but the reception was still manned, so he went and asked for Miriam Clarke.

After a short delay, the receptionist told him that Miriam was on her way down, and true enough, a few minutes later she emerged through the turnstiles.

"Hello, Inspector," she said extending her hand, "what can we do for you today?"

"Hi, Miriam. I just wanted to have another quick look in Mr Farrelly's office, if I may. It won't take a minute."

"Yes, OK. What are you looking for? We haven't touched it since you were here last."

"Just a quick shuftie. It shouldn't take long. Is everyone finishing early today, or what?" he said, changing the subject.

"Yes, Mr Mitchell has told everyone they can go at four if they want to. There's a function on later and he wants to give people a chance to get home and get changed into their glad rags."

"Are you going, Miriam?"

"No. I just can't. I'm very bad company at the moment. This thing with Jim has upset me a lot. I'm not in the humour for partying."

As they made their way towards Farrelly's office, Burke said, "Were you and he very close?"

"It was a purely professional relationship, if that's what you're getting at, Inspector, but yes, I guess you could say that. Jim was an excellent lawyer, and a kind man too. It's an unusual combination. Most of the other partners are right bastards."

Burke was a little taken aback by the woman's candidness, but tried not to show it.

"Is this where you sit?" Burke said as they passed a desk a few metres away from Farrelly's office.

"Yes. In between Jim and Martin Walsh. He's the other partner I look after."

Miriam busied herself locating the key for Farrelly's office and opening the door. Burke hung back a little, thinking that the woman had probably stashed her handbag on the floor near her desk. As she was busy opening the door, Burke pressed the call button on his phone discreetly which would initiate a call to Farrelly's unknown contact. But he could hear no ringing, although his own phone indicated that the connection had been made.

Burke made it look as if he was looking for something specific, but after a few minutes brought the subterfuge to a halt.

"Well, that's me done, Miriam. Thanks for your help. Can I ask you to make sure that the room is locked up again?"

"Yes, of course."

As they walked together back towards the lift, Kendron Mitchell appeared in the corridor.

"Ah, Inspector Burke, I heard you were on the premises. Can we have a word?"

"Yes, of course."

Mitchell dismissed Miriam Clarke and ushered Burke into his own office. When they were both seated, Mitchell began, "I just thought that you should know that AMRAAL have terminated their arrangements with us. They apparently felt that the passing of Jim Farrelly could affect them adversely in some way with regard to their licence application to the Irish authorities, so they have moved their business to another firm nearby."

"Oh. I'm sorry to hear that, Mr Mitchell. But I'm sure you have many other clients that can fill the gap."

"That's not quite the point, Inspector. AMRAAL was a flagship client for us. We were hoping to use the work we were doing for them to leverage other big pharma companies to join us. I need hardly tell you that that would have generated a very significant revenue stream for us. Indeed, AMRAAL itself contributed some fifteen percent of our annual billing as it was."

"Well, as I say, I'm sorry to hear that, but I'm not sure how I can help with any of that. I'm just intent on finding out who murdered Jim and his wife."

Mitchell raised an eyebrow.

"Are you certain the wife was murdered too, Inspector? Was it not just a nasty car accident? Poor Mrs Farrelly must have been in a very distressed state after her husband died in such a manner."

"Oh yes, we are quite certain. I can't go into the details, but there is compelling evidence of foul play."

"I see. Well, it's just that if you were able to apprehend the perpetrator quickly, and it turned out to be nothing to do with the firm, we might be able to rescue the AMRAAL situation. They probably would not give us everything, but we might be able to get back on terms with them and do some of their low-level work. Keep a foot in the door, as it were."

"I can assure you, Mr Mitchell, nothing would please me more than to catch the bugger that did this – and today, if possible. But so far, I can tell you without breaking any confidences, we've drawn a blank. So, if you don't mind, I'd like to get on with it. I'll let you know if anything significant develops."

Burke left the offices, and on his way back to his car, he mused silently, "They're all heart these bloody solicitors!"

Chapter Twenty-One

Amy Sutton walked over to where Fiona Moore was seated staring into a PC screen.

"Got a minute, Sarge?" she said.

"Sure, Amy. What's up?"

"The inspector asked me to check up on Jim Farrelly's flights with European Airways over the past three months. They got back to me just now, and there's something decidedly odd going on."

"Oh, what's that then?" Moore said.

"Look here. Farrelly flies out to London on a Monday, with his return ticket booked for the last flight back on Wednesday. Nothing odd there. But he books other flights using a different credit card to come back to Dublin on Monday evening, and then flies back out to London on the first flight out Tuesday, and the same on Tuesday night and Wednesday morning!"

"Cripes! He must be collecting air miles or something," Moore said.

"What do you make of it, boss?"

"I'm not sure. I wonder if Mrs Farrelly knew about this. Pity we can't check with her."

"Yes, it is. But who does that, for heaven's sake? It's nuts."

"Unless of course you are having a secret liaison with someone in Dublin and you don't want the missus to find out," Moore said.

"Gosh, I hadn't thought of that. I guess it would make sense, kinda. Seems like a lot of hassle to go to though for a bit of rumpy pumpy though," Amy Sutton said.

"You'd be surprised at the lengths men will go to for just that reason, Amy. Trust me, I know," Moore said, thinking of her boss and the Swedish pilot. "Anyway, I have to go out to Sheila Ward's place again. Fancy it?"

"Yeah, sure. Just let me get my jacket."

* * *

Fiona Moore and Amy Sutton drove out to Kinsealy, arriving at a few minutes past five. Sheila Ward arrived at exactly the same time, and when Mrs Ward had opened the gates, they drove in convoy to the front of the house.

"Good afternoon, Mrs Ward. I'm sorry to call unannounced, but I was wondering if we could have a word?" Moore said as they got out of their respective vehicles.

"Yes, I suppose so. I've been in town doing some shopping. Just essentials," the woman said, almost apologetically, "you'd better come in."

Sheila Ward opened the door of her house and tapped numbers into the alarm keypad to which it responded in a metallic voice, 'system unset'.

"Would you like a cup of tea, ladies? I'm parched."

"Yes, thanks, that would be lovely," Moore answered for the two of them.

Moore watched as her host placed her handbag on the island in the centre of the capacious kitchen. While Ward was occupied filling the kettle and getting down three mugs for their drinks, Moore nodded to Amy Sutton who she had primed on the way out in the car. Sutton pressed the call button on her own phone which was already loaded with the mystery number from Jim Farrelly's device. As the kettle came to the boil, a slightly muffled chirping struck up from inside Sheila Ward's handbag.

Sheila Ward turned around quickly, dropping the teaspoons that she had been holding on the floor and literally dived for her bag. Sutton cancelled the call, and the phone in the woman's handbag stopped before she had retrieved it.

"I think we need to talk, Mrs Ward," Moore said to the woman who was now looking rather furtive.

Sheila Ward pulled out a kitchen chair and more or less collapsed into it, all thoughts of preparing tea now forgotten.

Moore sat opposite her and waited.

"I suppose you know, then," Sheila said.

"Know what, Mrs Ward?"

"About Jim and me."

"All we know so far is that Mr Farrelly had a phone on him when he died that appeared to be used to call just one number. The number of the phone in your handbag. Would you care to explain?"

Sheila Ward let out a long sigh.

"Jim and I were having an affair. I know, it disgusts me even saying it now, but it wasn't like that. He was a really lovely guy, and he and Brenda had been going through a bad patch. It started one night when he was coming back from London early, and he stopped by to see me. He was very upset, and I suppose I wanted to comfort him. We ended up in bed. God! This is awful..." She started to sob softly.

Amy Sutton got up and completed the tea-making duties, bringing three mugs back to the table with a container of milk from the fridge.

"Do you take sugar, Mrs Ward?" Sutton said.

"What? Oh, no thanks. This is fine." She managed a tearful smile.

Moore let the atmosphere settle down a little and they all sipped their tea before she ventured further with her questions.

"Did Brenda Farrelly know any of this?" Moore asked.

"Heavens, no. We went to a lot of trouble to keep it just between us. Jim used to tell her he was going to London for three days, and then sneak back here on the in-between nights. He even used to hire a car at the airport in case Brenda got sight of his parking ticket or something. We were very careful, and to be honest, I'm not proud of myself, but these things happen, I suppose."

"Are you sure no one else knew anything about this?" Moore said.

"As sure as I can be. You can see we haven't really got any close neighbours here, and the house isn't overlooked. I'm pretty much a loner, although I do have friends, of course, but we generally meet away from the house in a restaurant or an hotel. And as I say, we were very careful."

"Had you and Jim got any plans?" Sutton said.

"Plans? What do you mean?"

"Were you planning on getting together permanently, or anything?"

"Oh, God, no. Jim would never do that to Brenda. Despite our affair, he loved her very much, and he would never hurt her. Nor would I, Sergeant. She was my sister after all."

"So, you never talked about what might happen if Jim was a free man, you know, single again?" Moore said.

"No! We did not! Are you implying that I might have had something to do with Brenda's accident?"

Sheila Ward had gone red in the face, and her hands were trembling a little.

"We're not suggesting anything at all, Mrs Ward. But we have to ask these questions. We have what looks like two rather nasty killings on our hands, after all, and what you have told us could be very relevant," Moore said.

"How do you mean, 'relevant'?"

"I'll be candid with you, Mrs Ward. Up to now, we have been unable to establish any possible motive for this double killing. What you have told us may change that, at least as far as Brenda Farrelly's death is concerned. Are you sure there's nothing more you want to disclose?"

"No, there bloody isn't. And I strongly resent what you are suggesting. I'd like you to leave now please, and if you want to talk to me again, I'll have a solicitor present. OK?" she said, challenging Moore to respond.

"Of course. That's not a problem, in fact I was about to recommend it myself. Right, we'll leave you to it then," Moore said, getting up from the table.

* * *

"What do you make of that?" Amy Sutton said as they drove back down along the Malahide Road towards town.

"To be honest, I had an inkling that it might have been the case, but I couldn't say anything to Burke. He'd have torn strips off me if I suggested such a thing without some corroboration."

"Well, we have that now. I suppose we should have lifted that mobile phone. I hope she doesn't destroy it," Sutton said.

"She won't. It has voicemails from Jim on it. She'll cling to it like an old photograph, and listen to his messages over and over in the wee small hours when she's crying herself to sleep."

"Crikey, Sarge. Ever thought of writing chick lit novels?" Sutton said.

"Feck off, Amy," she replied, smiling broadly.

Chapter Twenty-Two

Burke was holding court in the open office with his team.

"What Fiona and Amy have discovered about Sheila Ward and Jim Farrelly has changed the position quite substantially. We now appear to have what could be a motive for Jim's death, in any case. Though I can't quite see how it can account for Brenda Farrelly's killing. Any ideas?" he said, casting his eyes around the room.

"I wonder if it's possible that we are dealing with two separate crimes, boss? You know, Jim Farrelly's death having something to do with the affair, and Brenda Farrelly's killing being something else entirely, as yet unknown?" Dónal Lawler said.

"Hmm… but that would be an extraordinary coincidence, don't you think, Dónal? And you know what I think about those."

"Yes, sure, boss, but it does kinda make sense, doesn't it?" Lawler said, keen not to be put down quite so readily in front of the rest of the team.

"Maybe. But if that's the case, then we are missing something big in Brenda Farrelly's background. Tomorrow Fiona and I will go out to Naas to interview Peter Ward at his electronics factory. Amy, can you do a deep dive into

Brenda Farrelly? Bank accounts, phone records, know associates – the lot. And have a look at that dashcam footage again too. See how far back it goes, and if it reveals anything significant. If you don't find something, we may have to get a warrant to search the Farrelly home again, and the Super is already up my arse about lack of progress on this case, so don't let me down. OK?"

"Yes, boss," Sutton said.

"Dónal, how did you get on looking into the background of the flight attendants on Farrelly's flights? Remember, we have to interview them tomorrow night out at the airport."

"Not too good, to be honest, sir. It's very difficult with these Eastern Europeans, and they are all from different countries too."

"Have you enlisted the help of Europol?"

"Yes, sir, but although they are trying to be helpful, it's very slow. They have to contact the local police in each of the countries the girls come from and as I understand it, cooperation isn't exactly forthcoming."

"Use these two English words to make a well-known phrase or saying, Dónal, 'backside' and 'rocket'. Get it?"

"Yes, sir, I hear you."

"Good man. Right. That's it for tonight. If we're not in touch before, let's meet here at five o'clock tomorrow for a briefing on the interviews. Dónal will have full chapter and verse on the four ladies by then, I'm sure!"

"Yes, sir," they said in unison.

* * *

Back in his office on his own, Burke saw that he had a message on his mobile phone from a number starting with 0046. He listened to the voicemail.

"Hi, Aidan, it's Andrea. Give me a call when you get a moment. Thanks. Bye."

Despite himself, Burke felt a few butterflies cruising around in his gut at the sound of the woman's voice. He didn't hesitate before returning the call.

"Hi, Andrea. I thought you would be at 35,000 feet over somewhere at this time. Everything OK?"

"Yes, sure, but we had a problem on the flight to the Canaries. There was a problem with the plane and we had to go into Madrid. By the time they discovered what was wrong, Piotr and I were going out of hours to complete the flights, so they got another crew and we flew back to Gatwick."

"Gosh, was that a bit scary for you?"

"No, not really. It was just an indicator from the left-hand engine saying it was overheating, so we shut it down and landed on one. It's perfectly safe. Anyway, it's usually the electronics and not the engine at all. We are well trained to cope."

"Yes, I'm sure you are. Anyway, how are you, apart from that?"

"Good. Listen, I was wondering if you'd like to come over to Sweden on Saturday for the weekend? I'm flying over on Saturday morning, and there's a flight from Dublin that gets in around the same time. I could meet you at the airport."

"Is that Arlanda?"

"Yes, of course. I can get you a ticket too, if you like, but maybe you are too busy," Andrea said, her voice sounding a little despondent as she gave Burke an out.

"No, not at all. Well, of course we are busy, but I can take Saturday and Sunday off. It would be fun!"

"Great! I'll send the ticket to your phone, and I'll meet you in the arrivals at Arlanda at around eleven-thirty. I'll text if there is any delay, but I doubt it on a Saturday."

"Lovely. Thanks, Andrea. I'm looking forward to seeing you."

"Yes, me too. See you Saturday then. Bye."

"Bye, love."

Burke's humour was greatly improved as a result of the phone call. So much so, that he decided to call it a day, even though it wasn't even six o'clock. He went across the road to the local pub and ordered a pint of Guinness. As he sat on a stool at the bar, he brought up a photo of Andrea Bergin he had taken in Trinity College with her standing in front of the Campanile. He pinched two fingers on the screen to bring her face up close.

"God, I'm a lucky bastard," he said to himself as the barman placed the black drink with a creamy head down in front of him.

* * *

Burke was still in good spirits the following morning as he and Fiona Moore headed for Naas to interview Peter Ward. He had downed just the one pint of stout in the pub opposite Store Street Garda station and driven home the previous night still smiling about his good fortune. Once at home, he had carefully ironed two of his best shirts, and packed a small suitcase with other essentials for his weekend away.

"You're in good form, boss. Anything planned for the weekend?" Moore said, yielding to her gut instinct as to the source of her bosses elevated demeanour.

Burke glanced sideways at his colleague wondering how the hell she had figured that out.

"Actually, I'll be away. You'll be OK to hold the fort, I hope. I'll be back Sunday night in any case."

"Sure, no problem. Going anywhere nice?" she said mischievously.

"Ah, no, just getting out of the city for a bit. You know how it is."

"Yeah, of course," she said, realising that further pursuit of the boss's leisure activities would not be wise. In any case, they were at the outskirts of Naas and Moore needed to navigate them to the premises of Power Electronic Devices. Moore had checked the website for directions, and noted that the word 'Power' had a capital P and a capital W in the logo, reflecting the ownership of Peter Ward.

They stopped in front of the grey metal-clad building, which looked very much like all the others in the little business park, and got out. Inside, it was a different story. The reception area which bristled with the very latest technology was on the first floor, and there was a dark-haired girl seated behind an expansive desk on which was parked a huge Apple computer screen.

The girl asked how she could help, and Moore told her that they had come to see Mr Ward.

"Ah, yes, he's expecting you. I'll just tell him you are here."

This she managed to do without lifting a handset, but simply by pressing a button on a tiny device that was lodged in her ear, under her hair.

Moore looked at Burke and raised her eyebrows.

"He will be with you in a moment. Can I get you a tea or coffee?"

"Thanks, that would be lovely. Two coffees please, no sugar, just a drop of milk," Burke said, answering for both of them, and wondering what technological marvel would be pressed into service to deliver the beverages.

The receptionist didn't move, or speak to anyone, but about a minute later another woman emerged from behind a panel at the back of the area carrying a tray with two tall glass mugs filled with coffee and a small plate of wrapped chocolate biscuits.

"Thanks," Burke said, somewhat mesmerized by the arrangement.

They were about halfway through their drinks, when the receptionist addressed them again.

"You can go through now, Inspector. Take your drinks with you if you like."

Again, Burke was puzzled. The girl hadn't seemed to speak to anyone, and he wondered how on earth she had received the instruction to admit them to Peter Ward's office.

Chapter Twenty-Three

Peter Ward was a tall, slim, good-looking man in his very late forties or early fifties. He was neatly dressed in chinos with a linen jacket, a well-ironed button-down shirt, and casual brown loafers. His hair, a kind of salt-and-pepper colour, was neatly trimmed and he was clean-shaven.

"Come in, folks, take a seat," Ward said as the two detectives entered the room via an electrically operated sliding door.

Ward's office was large and uncluttered. Behind his desk, which had nothing but another large Apple computer on it, there were huge plate-glass windows that provided a view of the factory floor below. The factory was comprised of three large rooms, each with a different-coloured metal surround at the entrance. The units had a kind of airlock arrangement at the door, so that personnel entering did not contaminate the interior, and everyone working inside there was clad in clean suits, so that they looked like some kind of zombie army as they moved slowly and deliberately around.

Burke walked over to the glass and looked down.

"Impressive, Mr Ward. What exactly do you make here?" he said.

"We manufacture electronic components for various companies such as IBM and Intel. We also do work for some of the more advanced automotive companies such as Tesla and Nio, but that's top secret, I'm afraid."

"I see. As I said, very impressive," Burke said, turning back to the office and taking a seat beside his colleague.

"How can I help you today then?" Ward said to them both.

"We're here to talk about the death of Jim Farrelly and his wife, Mr Ward. I understand you are, or were, related to them in some way."

"Oh, yes. Very tragic, very tragic indeed. Poor Jim just having a heart attack like that. Still, I suppose we know not the day nor the hour as they say."

"What makes you say it was a heart attack, Mr Ward?"

"Well, wasn't it? It's what most highly stressed businessmen die of, after all."

"No, it wasn't. Mr Farrelly was murdered with a particularly nasty poison. His last hours must have been agony for him. We're investigating his death, and that of his poor wife too," Burke said.

"Wife! I thought she died in a car accident."

"Tell me, Mr Ward, without betraying any trade secrets, what sort of components do you manufacture for the automotive industry?" Moore said.

"They are mostly highly reliable temperature control units. These new electric cars are prone to overheating, so keeping them cool is vital to avoid fires. That's our speciality. We make control units for IBM and Intel too, for their servers, which also have to be kept at the right temperature to function correctly."

"Really, how so?" Burke asked.

"Well, if a computer or a server gets too hot, its calculations can become unreliable. With double precision maths, even an error at the fifteenth decimal place can be disastrous for the end user, so temperature has to be carefully controlled," Ward said.

"Do any of these components end up in the cruise control mechanisms of cars?" Moore said.

"I doubt it, although we don't specify what the customer does with them after we have supplied them, but it's very unlikely. As far as I know, cruise control is all about regulating fuel flow to the engine, not temperature."

"Yes, but could they be modified to do that, do you think?" Burke added.

"I really have no idea. Look, Inspector, what's this all really about? I mean if you say Farrelly was poisoned and his wife died in a car crash, what on earth do you think I can tell you that will help you sort it out?"

"How well did you know the Farrellys, Mr Ward?" Moore said.

"Not terribly. I used to be married to Sheila, as I'm sure you know. Sheila is Brenda's sister. We used to get together at Christmas, birthdays, that sort of thing. But we weren't close. Jim was always too busy to socialize much."

"Were you aware that Jim Farrelly and your ex-wife were having an affair?" Burke said.

"What? That's nonsense. Who told you that? Sheila wouldn't. She's not the type, and neither was Jim. It's ridiculous."

"Ridiculous maybe, but true all the same. Sheila told us herself – eventually," Burke said.

"Are you sure you didn't know about this?" Moore said.

"Yes, I bloody am. Why? What do you think? I got jealous over the antics of a woman I have no affection for anymore and bumped off her lover in some sort of revenge killing? Is that what you think? You've been reading too many fantasy novels, Inspector."

"Mr Ward, we have been trying hard to establish a motive for these killings, and frankly, without a lot of success. But jealousy among partners, ex or not, often features in this type of case. So, we have to ask these questions – like it or not," Burke said.

"Well, I don't like it. Not one bit. You have no right to come in here bandying accusations about like that. I've a good mind to file a complaint," Ward said, but they could see by his expression that he had no intention of so doing. "Now, if that's all, I have a busy day ahead. Can you see yourselves out?"

Moore wasn't prepared to give up so easily.

"Are you telling us that you have no idea who might have been responsible for these murders, Mr Ward, and you knew nothing of your ex-wife's affair with Jim Farrelly?"

"That's exactly what I am saying. And I have nothing more to add, so would you please leave."

Moore looked at Burke who just shrugged, and the two of them got up and left as instructed.

* * *

"What do you reckon?" Moore said as Burke drove down the slip road onto the N7 heading back to town.

"I dunno. He's a cool customer, that's for sure, but it seems like a dead end. I can't see him having any connection to ricin or any means of delivering it, to be honest. But I'll tell you one thing. I bet he cuts off Sheila Ward's allowance after that bombshell we left him with."

"God. I hope not. She seems like a nice woman, and it's not her fault her husband traded her in for a younger model," Moore said.

"Yeah, but screwing your sister's husband isn't very nice, is it?"

"Maybe not. But who are we to judge? People get tangled up in all sorts of unsuitable relationships," Moore said, and her comment hung in the air for the rest of the journey back to the Garda station.

As they entered the building, Burke's phone pinged. He glanced at the screen. It was his ticket from Dublin to Arlanda arriving from Andrea. He smiled broadly as he put the device back in his pocket.

Chapter Twenty-Four

The team came together as arranged to discuss the upcoming interviews with the flight crew that had worked the flights on the fateful day that Jim Farrelly had been found dead in seat 14F.

"Dónal, have you got anything back on the background checks on the cabin crew?"

"No. Sorry, boss. They say it will be tomorrow at the earliest. I tried to hurry them along, but there's a lot of red tape."

"Damn! OK. Never mind, it's not your fault, Dónal. We'll just have to fly by the seat of our pants, as it were."

They all moaned at Burke's feeble pun.

"Right, well, when we get out there, I'll liaise with that guy, Rory, he's been very helpful. I'll ask him to arrange four separate areas for us to work, and we'll take one each. I'll talk to Marta, the senior hostess. Fiona, Dónal, Amy, you can divide up the other three to suit yourselves. OK?" Burke said.

"Yes, boss, fine. What exactly are we looking for?" Amy Sutton said.

"We have to be careful not to treat them like suspects. Just ask them about the day that Farrelly died. I understand they were on his outbound flight early in the morning, so maybe on that leg, one of them noticed him. It would have been a good deal quieter at that time of the morning. Be thorough. I want details. That's the best way to see if there's complete consistency across the four of them."

"Should we ask about the flight crew too, boss?" Dónal said.

"Well, only if there was any interaction between the cabin attendants and the flight crew. But they've told me they focus on flying the damn thing and have very little if anything to do with the cabin, but ask away. Contrary to what you might think, those planes don't actually fly themselves. At that hour there's a lot of traffic going west to east over the UK, and I understand that there is a lot of radio work, and so on. I imagine the flight crew were fairly well occupied. Right, let's get moving. Can we take at least two cars? I need to get away smartly after."

* * *

The four of them arrived at the airport in a convoy of three cars, and parked as was their habit, right in front of the terminal. Burke went to the European Airways desk in arrivals and asked for Rory Dillon, and a few moments later, the man appeared dressed in his high-vis yellow jacket and carrying the inevitable clipboard.

"Good evening, Inspector," Dillon said extending his hand.

"Hi, Rory. How's things?" Burke said.

"All good. I have the four girls waiting in separate rooms that crew use when they are delayed. They are small, but they do the job. I've put an extra chair in each as well so you can sit with them face to face, otherwise one of you would have to sit on the bed. Hardly appropriate."

"That's great, Rory. Thanks for your help," Burke said as Dillon led the way down through a labyrinth of narrow corridors away from the public areas.

After a few minutes they arrived at a series of doors labelled 'C201', 'C202' and so on.

"There ya go. Give me a shout when you're done. This lot have to be away in just over two hours, so it would be great if you could finish by then. I get a right bollocking if the flight doesn't depart on schedule."

"That's no problem, Rory. We probably won't be any longer than half an hour. Which room is Marta in?"

"Here, C201," Dillon said, nodding to the nearest door.

"Right, thanks. See you in a while."

Burke knocked on the door and entered. Marta was sitting in one of the chairs dressed in her uniform, but she had let her hair down and appeared to be quite relaxed.

"Thanks very much for this, Marta. I'm Detective Inspector Burke. I just wanted to have a chat with you about the flights that you operated on the day Mr Farrelly died. I'm sure you remember the day well."

"I'll never ever forget it, Inspector. Take a seat."

"Thanks. Firstly, may I ask how long you have been with European Airways?"

"Of course. I joined four years ago. They had a recruitment drive on in Gdansk, and they were holding interviews. I was working in a café at that time. I saw their ads and applied. After two interviews and a practical examination, I was given the job, and here we are," the young woman said, spreading out her hands in front of her.

"Your English is perfect, Marta. Did you have to learn that for the job?"

"No, Inspector. I speak fluent German, French, Polish of course, English, and I have a smattering of Russian. I also have a degree in European Languages from the University of Gdansk at Masters level."

"Interesting. You must be clever too," Burke said.

"Not especially. I work hard though."

"But could you not get a better job maybe as an interpreter at the European Commission or United Nations or something with those qualifications?"

"Probably. But I like my job. Despite what you hear, European Airways are good employers, and the perks are good. Free seats all over their network. We do long hours when we are working, but we get a lot of time off, and I can get seats if they are empty for my family too. My parents have been to Greece and Spain. They would never have done that if I was working in an office."

"Tell me what you remember about the early morning flight from Dublin to Gatwick that day, Marta."

"It was fairly busy. We got into Dublin at around 7:15 and we were due out again at 8:10. We didn't have to load fuel, so it was just a matter of deplaning the inbound passengers, doing a quick clean-up on the cabin and then boarding the new passengers. The other girls looked after most of it. I spent the time on the flight deck talking to Piotr and Andrea till just before departure."

"Are you friendly with them?"

"Yes, a little. We work quite a lot together, and Piotr is very amusing. He has some crazy stories about when he was in the Turkish Air Force. He flew one of their 737 early warning and reconnaissance machines. He had some very hairy experiences over Russia. But, anyway, yes, about the day of the flight. It was perfectly normal. A few people looking for alcohol, but mostly just breakfast rolls, and hot drinks. We did the cabin service in about thirty-five minutes and then had time to offer them the dreaded scratch cards and duty-free stuff which no one purchased."

"Does anyone ever win anything on those things?"

"Oh, yes, they do. I was on a flight last month when a passenger won €10,000. It was a riot!"

"Marta, tell me, do any of the cabin crew ever bring anything on board that they sell to the passengers for themselves?"

"How do you mean?"

"Oh, I don't know, extra food, sandwiches or something, or chocolate bars, or even perfume."

Marta flushed a little, and changed her position in her seat.

"I've never seen it, but I have heard of it happening all right. Of course, it's instant dismissal if you are caught. The company has a very tight stock control system, and it would have to be cash only. Most of the passengers tap with their cards these days, so it would be very difficult."

"Have you worked much with the other girls on the flight?"

"Yes, we are often rostered together. They are great to work with. I never have any trouble."

"So, on the day in question, there was nothing at all unusual about the outbound flight. What about the return later that night?"

"You mean the last flight Gatwick to Dublin?"

"Yes, the one where we found Mr Farrelly dead in his seat."

"That was mad as usual. Very busy. We had a stag party and two hen parties going to Dublin for the weekend and they consumed every drop of alcohol we were carrying. They were a noisy lot too. Andrea was flying, and she put the boot down, so it only lasted just short of fifty minutes. She told me that in the evening they can take a short cut across South Wales and the Irish Sea where the RAF have it closed off during the day. It puts a lot of pressure on us though, but we managed."

"And again, you didn't notice anything at all unusual about the flight?"

"No. Well, there was one thing that I thought was a bit odd."

"What was that, Marta?"

"About halfway across I was called to the flight deck. I thought they probably wanted a coffee or something, but no. Andrea left to use the toilet. It's quite unusual for the Pilot Flying to do that on a short flight, and of course one pilot cannot be left alone in the cockpit anymore after that terrible German thing."

"Was she away long?"

"No, that's the funny thing. She was back almost immediately. But I was so busy, I didn't pay any attention. I was glad to get back to the madness and finish off service."

"OK, Marta, thank you very much for your help. I won't keep you any longer. You'll need to prepare for your next flight. Here's my phone number if you think of anything else that might help," Burke said handing her his card.

"Have you discovered what happened yet?"

"No, not yet, Marta, but we are making progress," Burke said, then got up and left the room.

* * *

Burke made his way back out to the main airport concourse, and was getting a coffee from one of the outlets when the other three appeared.

"Coffee, anyone?"

"No thanks," they said in turn.

"So, how did that go?"

"Not very well," Fiona Moore said. "There was nothing unusual about either the outbound flight in the morning, or the inbound one later as far as the girls are concerned. I did learn one thing from Sally though."

"Oh. What's that then?" Burke said.

"The senior stewardess shares a small flat with the pilot girl, Bergin, close to Gatwick. It's not their home, but they bunk down there during the week when they are flying in and out."

"What! You mean Marta?" Burke said.

"Yes, that's her. They have shared for over a year now, Sally said."

"Bugger!" Burke said.

"What, boss?" Moore said.

"I've just spent half an hour interviewing Marta, and I never managed to extract that little nugget of information from her."

Moore tried very hard to keep a straight face, and Amy Sutton and Dónal Lawler had to look away.

"Oh well. Never mind. We know now in any case. And maybe Marta just didn't want you to know. Obviously, Andrea hasn't said anything to you about it," Moore said.

"What? No, no she hasn't."

Chapter Twenty-Five

The flight from Dublin to Sweden was uneventful. Andrea had reserved one of the seats with extra legroom for Burke halfway along the cabin next to the over-wing emergency doors, and as the aircraft headed north towards Scandinavia, Burke dozed off, enjoying the luxury of the extra space. He hadn't been to Sweden previously. Before he was separated, he and his wife travelled on holiday almost every year, but that was south to the sun. They had visited Majorca several times, and had been to Ibiza and even as far as Corfu one year, though that didn't go well due to very bad weather. So he was looking forward to seeing what Sweden had to offer.

The first thing he noticed about the airport was the cleanliness of the place. Dublin Airport was clean, but this was in a different league. He observed dozens of cleaners polishing the floors, the expansive windows, the handrails and even the moving walkways as he made his way from the gate to the baggage hall and out into the arrivals area.

As soon as he appeared, he spotted Andrea who walked over and put her arms around him before planting a kiss on his willing lips.

"Welcome to Sweden, Aidan. How was your flight?"

"Great thanks. And thanks for arranging the extra legroom. Much appreciated," he said, squeezing her hand.

"All part of the service!" She smiled.

"How about your flight? Was that OK too?" Burke asked as they strolled towards the exit.

"I had to work it, hence the uniform. The pilot called in sick this morning, so I volunteered. They even put me in the left-hand seat this time. The other guy looked about fifteen to me and he was dead nervous. I don't know if that was because I'm a woman, or whether he was just very new to the job. But he did OK."

"Exciting. Have you a car here, Andrea, or do we get a taxi?"

"I have my car, but unlike you, I can't park directly in front of the terminal. But it's not far."

As they walked across to the Swedavia car park, Burke asked his companion, "Where are we going?"

"I need to go home and change out of my work clothes. Then maybe we should look for some lunch. There are plenty of cafés and restaurants near where I live."

"Sounds good," Burke said.

Andrea Bergin's car was a sleek Mercedes CLA model, and by the look of the shine on the paintwork, and the general condition of the vehicle, it was quite new.

"Nice car," Burke said, as Andrea opened the boot to put her case in.

"A girl has to have some pleasures, don't you think?"

Burke smiled, but said nothing, getting into the passenger's seat on the right-hand side of the car and feeling a bit at sea with the left-hand drive arrangement.

Andrea drove briskly but safely out of the airport and towards the city. Burke could not get over how well ordered everything was. Again, the cleanliness of the place was obvious, and the traffic moved smartly but in a very disciplined way. There was no running red lights like he was used to in Dublin, and pedestrians waited for the green light to cross the road at intersections.

"I love this car, Andrea. Is it new?"

"Fairly. I got it in the springtime. I hope I'm not driving too fast."

"No, not at all. The traffic is very well behaved here. Not like Ireland," Burke said.

"I think it works better this way."

Andrea lived in a suburb of Stockholm on the airport side of town called Sollentuna. As she drove down the narrow street and approached her apartment building, she blipped a fob on the dashboard, and pulled up in front of steel gates that were slowly receding to allow her to drive in. She slotted her Mercedes in neatly between two other vehicles in what was obviously a designated parking slot and turned off the engine.

They retrieved their bags and went upstairs in the lift to the seventh floor of the building. Andrea used her key to open the door of apartment number 74, and they went in. The apartment was large and had lovely views out across the nearby cemetery to the sea. Burke figured it must have been nearly 100 square metres in all, including a generous terrace accessed by full-length sliding doors. It was furnished in the typical minimalist style that Sweden is known for. The furniture was nearly all pale in colour, and there was hardly a rounded edge to be seen anywhere. It reminded Burke of IKEA, but much more upmarket than that.

"Wow! This is some place, Andrea. Is it very expensive to rent?" Burke said, looking out at the view.

"I don't know. I actually own it myself," she said, coming over to join him at the window.

"Nice. European Airways must pay very well indeed," Burke said.

"C'mon, I need to change out of these clothes. You can unpack at the same time if you like," Andrea said, and they went together to one of the two bedrooms with a large double bed and an array of built-in wardrobes.

* * *

Moore arrived at Store Street Garda station just before ten on the Saturday morning. Once again, she was disappointed that Burke had taken off and left her to it. But today she at least had the help of Amy Sutton and Dónal Lawler. When they had all got a cup of coffee, they sat around in a circle to discuss the case.

"Just let's do a bit of brainstorming for a few minutes, guys, see if we can't come up with some new angles. Dónal, you go first," Moore said.

"OK, Sarge. Well, I've been thinking. It's just possible that we are looking at two entirely separate crimes here. I know the boss doesn't like coincidences, and all that, but it seems to me that the motives for killing Jim Farrelly and the motive for killing his wife could be two totally different things."

"Hmm… OK, what's your theory?"

"I'd say Farrelly's murder was probably work-related. He must have found out something very negative about one of his clients that would have done them serious damage if it got out. So bad, in fact, that it was worth killing him," Lawler said.

"Right, Dónal, let's go with that for the moment. What about the wife?" Sutton said.

"I think that might be somehow connected to Peter Ward. His outfit makes car bits, after all," Lawler said.

"I see what you mean. Why don't we get back to forensics and see if they can trace the components of the device that was fitted to Brenda Farrelly's car. Find out who made them, then get onto the manufacturer and see if they supplied any of the same parts to Power Electronic Devices. But why would Peter Ward want to bump off his sister-in-law, Dónal? Unless of course there's a money dimension to all this. You know what the boss always says."

"Yeah, follow the money," Sutton said.

"What about if there was big life insurance at play here? We know Jim Farrelly had a big insurance policy through his firm. His doctor told us he had to go for check-ups regularly, that the insurance company insisted. If it was six or seven times earnings for death in service, it could amount to a few million," Moore said.

"OK, so Farrelly dies, presumably his estate goes to his wife, and then she dies as well, where does the money go then?" Lawler said.

"Exactly, Dónal, where? Tenner bets it goes to the sister, Sheila Ward. There aren't any kids anywhere, so logic dictates that Sheila is probably the main beneficiary," Moore said.

"Yes, and if the Wards aren't actually divorced, then Peter Ward could lay claim to half of his wife's money when they do finally get the *decree nisi*. Let's have a look at Ward's finances too. See if he is as well-heeled as he appears. Oh, and I've just had a ghastly thought. If Ward has already killed, maybe twice, he might not want to wait around for the divorce. Sheila Ward could be in mortal danger," Lawler said.

"Christ! What a mess. But we can't just go barging in and tell her that her husband is about to murder her. We'll just have to hope that he isn't in too much of a hurry for the cash, if our theory is correct. Dónal, will you follow up with forensics? Amy, you can dig into the insurance issue and the Farrellys' wills on Monday when everyone is back at work. I'm going to do a deep dive on Power Electronic Devices, see what I can find out."

* * *

Dónal Lawler was lucky to get hold of Daniel in forensics on a Saturday. He was putting in some overtime, just like the detectives, and he was on his own in the lab when Lawler's call came through.

"Hi, Dónal. I guess you're putting in the hours too. How can I help?" Daniel said.

Lawler asked him to start tracking down the component manufacturers from the device that they had recovered from Brenda Farrelly's car.

"Sure, no problem. In fact, I think we've already started that. But while you're on, there's something else. I've been doing a bit more work on Farrelly's laptop. I found a few hidden folders stashed away in a thing called a vault. It's arranged so that it doesn't show up in the normal directory listing. You have to tell it to reveal hidden files, and voilà."

"Interesting. What's in the files, Daniel?"

"One of them is called 'Notes to self'. There are a series of notes with some kind of code and a few very cryptic words. I haven't time to figure it all out. Can I send it over to you?"

"Yes, of course. I'll spend some time on it this afternoon. Thanks."

Chapter Twenty-Six

On Sunday morning Andrea and her guest got up shortly before ten o'clock. While Burke was in the shower, Andrea prepared breakfast with lots of piping hot coffee. They both tucked into scrambled eggs, followed by croissants and jam.

"This is lovely, Andrea. Thanks for looking after me so well. Listen, I hope you don't mind me asking, but how the hell can you afford all this?" he said, sweeping his arm around in an arc towards the seating area of the expansive open plan apartment.

"I mean, nothing in here is budget, and then there's your car as well. Call me a nosey parker, but I'm curious."

"It's no mystery, Aidan. The airline pays me well. I have no responsibilities except to myself. I spend all I earn because I like nice things. That's it."

"You're right, too. Unfortunately, I was married previously, and I still have to support my ex-wife. That doesn't leave much over for spoiling myself, I'm afraid. I don't even own that modest little house where you stayed. It's mortgaged up to the hilt."

Andrea reached across the table and covered Burke's hand.

"Don't worry about it, Aidan. Money isn't everything. But tell me, are you happy?"

"Right now, yes, very." He smiled at her as he squeezed her hand.

"Listen, love, I have to go out for about an hour. I have some private business to attend to. Will you be OK here on your own till I get back?" Andrea said.

"Yes, of course. I'll be fine. Off you go."

Andrea dressed in expensive clothes and asked Burke if he wanted a spare key in case he wanted to go for a walk.

"No, it's fine. I'll just stay here, if that's OK, and chill."

"Sure. Whatever suits. I'll see you in a while."

Andrea kissed him, and then she was gone.

Burke stood at the window and watched as Andrea's car pulled out of the underground car park onto the street. She accelerated away quickly, turned left at the end of the street and disappeared from view.

As soon as Burke was happy that she was really out of the way, he started to look around the apartment. Something wasn't right. This woman had far too much money, and it made him nervous. He started in her bedroom. He was very accustomed to carrying out a search of a premises without the occupant knowing what had taken place. He went through her wardrobe where he found more expensive clothes, and then to her dressing table where one of the drawers contained Andrea's personal papers. He rifled through them quickly, but found nothing untoward. He was about to go and search the living room when he spotted something odd about the bed. A long cotton valance covered the sides of the mattress right down to the floor, but behind the pleated fabric there were drawers. Burke lifted the valance, tucked it under the mattress and opened the first drawer. It was empty. The next drawer was more fruitful. As he pulled it towards him, he could see bundles of euro notes wrapped in coloured plastic packs. He didn't want to touch the money, and without counting it, he couldn't estimate how much was there, but he guessed there must be at least €50,000 stashed in the drawer.

"Shit, shit, shit!" he said out loud. "What the fuck have I got myself into?"

When he had collected his thoughts, Burke finished his search of the apartment but found nothing more of interest. He sat down on the sofa in the living room and took out his phone.

"Fiona, is that you?" he said.

"Yes, boss, of course. Where are you?"

"I'm in Stockholm. I'm staying with Andrea for the weekend, but I'll be back in Dublin later this evening. Listen, I want you to do something for me. Can you run a background check on Andrea Bergin and Piotr Kaan? Get as much as you can, and do it quickly."

"Yes, all right, boss. I'm in the office anyway. Are you OK?" Moore said.

"Yes, yes, I'm fine. It's just that... well... look, never mind, just do the background checks, will you, and don't call me back. I'll ring you when I reach home," he said. He hung up the phone.

Burke spent the next fifteen minutes making sure that Andrea would not notice what he had been up to in her absence, and a few minutes later, she arrived back.

"Sorry about that, love, I'm all yours now for the rest of the day," she said, snuggling up to him. "I thought you might like to do a canal tour. It's very scenic, and if we get the right boat, we can get lunch on board."

"Sounds great. Is it far from here?"

"No, not at all. Just a few minutes' walk. Get your jacket and let's go."

They spent the rest of their time together enjoying the sights of Stockholm, and they enjoyed a delicious lunch on board the canal barge. By three o'clock it was time for Burke to get to the airport. Andrea's flight back to Gatwick wasn't until later in the evening.

They stopped by at her apartment to collect his bag, and then Andrea drove to the airport. She pulled up outside the departures building, and Andrea leaned across. They kissed for what seemed like a long time, and when they disengaged, Andrea said, "Well, Mr Policeman, when am I going to see you again?"

"I'm sure we can work something out, love. Are you off next weekend?"

"Yes, I think so. I haven't seen the roster yet for the full week, but I'm sure it's just the same as every other week. I could probably come to Dublin like before, if you want."

"Of course I want. But I'm not sure how I'm fixed yet till I see what's going on at the station. Why don't I give you a call on Tuesday or so?"

"Yes, OK."

"Thanks, love. I'll just get my case from the boot, and then I'll be off."

He leaned across and kissed her again, and then got out of the car. As he went to the back of the car and opened the boot to retrieve his bag, he noticed that there was a small package wrapped in brown paper stuffed into one of the cubbies at the side of the luggage compartment that looked out of place in the pristine car.

* * *

When Burke got back to his somewhat down-at-heel house in Crumlin it was after seven o'clock. He poured himself a stiff whiskey, plonked himself down on the sofa, and took out his phone to call Fiona Moore.

"Hi, Fiona, it's me. Anything to report?"

Moore filled Burke in on the conversations that the team had had earlier in the day.

"Do you think Lawler could be right? This could be two entirely separate cases?" Moore said.

"I don't know, Fiona. Maybe. Did you get anywhere with the background checks on Bergin and Kaan?"

"No, not yet, boss. I've put the wheels in motion, but it is still Sunday after all. I should have something back tomorrow afternoon. Anyway, how was your weekend?"

"Interesting. I'll fill you in tomorrow. Thanks, Fiona, I'll leave you to it then. Goodnight."

"Goodnight, sir."

Chapter Twenty-Seven

There was a decidedly Monday morning feeling when the team assembled at nine o'clock in Store Street. It was a grey day, with thick, featureless clouds hanging over the city, and that light drizzle that isn't really rain, but soaks you to the skin in about five minutes all the same.

Takeaway coffees had been brought in by everyone, and the only bright spot was Burke's humour, which seemed to be in sharp contrast to the rest of them.

"Good Monday, everyone! How are we all this typical autumn day?"

A low murmur went around the room.

The team brought the inspector up to date with their work over the weekend.

"So, what have we found out from the hidden files on Farrelly's computer?"

"Not a lot, to be honest, sir. It seems to be some type of code he's been using. I had a look last night, but I haven't cracked it yet," Dónal Lawler said a little defensively.

"OK. Well, give me a look at it, and I'll see if anything occurs. Have we found out anything more about Farrelly's clients that might be of interest?"

"Yes, well sort of. I was researching AMRAAL, sir. It seems that there has been a lot of trouble over that Trebutivan drug. There's talk of rigged clinical trials and all sorts of nefarious goings-on related to it. That's why I think they want to move production to Ireland. Less oversight. If the drug gets delisted, then that's the end of AMRAAL," Amy Sutton said.

"Yes, and there's quite a few snippets from various newspapers and trade magazines on Farrelly's computer about it. They are nearly all small pieces buried deep in the publications. Often just a paragraph or two. It looks as if Farrelly was gathering information, though for what purpose, I'm not sure," Dónal said.

"Right, well I feel another visit to Kendron Mitchell coming on. But first, here's some other news to brighten up your week. As some of you know," Burke said, looking directly at Fiona Moore, "I was in Sweden at the weekend. During the trip, I visited Andrea Bergin's apartment."

"Lucky you," Lawler said with a broad grin which was quickly dealt with by a dirty look from the inspector.

"While Andrea was out, I had a look around, and I found a drawer packed full of cash in her bedroom. What do you make of that?"

They all looked at each other for inspiration, being conscious that they needed to respond carefully for the sake of their boss's dignity.

"It could be innocent enough," Amy Sutton ventured.

"Perhaps. But that's not all. Bergin is driving an almost new Mercedes CLA, and her apartment is more like that of a movie star than an overworked first officer. Amy, can you get on to the police in Stockholm directly. Let's bypass Europol on this occasion. Speak to a senior officer and find out if Bergin is known to them for any reason. If you need to, get the Super to open up the channel for you, but it probably won't be necessary."

"Right, boss, will do."

"And, Dónal, forward me yer man's cryptic notes, will you? I'll have a look at them now. Then, you and me, Fiona, are going visiting again."

"OK, boss. Milligan Walker by any chance?" Moore said.

"Now I know why they made you into a detective, Sergeant," he said, smiling.

"Oh, and, Dónal, follow up on the components in that device in Mrs Farrelly's car, will you? I have a feeling someone is pissing us about, and I don't like it."

"Yes, boss," Lawler said. Burke's early morning good humour appeared to be leaving him already, and it wasn't even ten o'clock.

* * *

Burke printed out the several pages that Dónal Lawler had sent him from Jim Farrelly's hidden notes.

996 2305 5 350
996 3005 4 250
995 0706 8 450 – Fri
996 1006 2 150

There were several more lines that looked similar.

Burke called Moore into his office.

"What do you make of these, Fiona?"

Moore studied the list for a moment.

"Well, the second set of numbers is obviously dates. Could the first group be flight numbers maybe? And I haven't a clue what the rest of it means."

"Hmm... I agree. But here's the odd thing. If they are days, the first three are all Fridays, but only the last one – 0706 – is noted as such. And it has a different first three numbers too."

"Yes, I spotted that. Is there a timestamp on the files at all?"

"Good point. Ask Dónal to bring in the laptop opened up at the hidden directory and we'll have a look."

Moore was back a few moments later with the little black Lenovo computer. Burke positioned it sideways on in front of them both, and started exploring the directory.

"Yes, look here. This one was last accessed at 08:35 on the day he died. He would have been in the air on his way to London at that time on the early morning flight," Burke said.

"And the cabin crew said that it was a quiet flight. Maybe someone spotted him doing something on his PC that they didn't like. I dunno, it's all a bit far-fetched for my liking though."

"I agree. Let's park it for now and go and see your friendly solicitor," Burke said.

"OK. Just let me get my jacket. Yours or mine?"

"Neither. We'll take a squad car. I want this taken seriously!"

* * *

The weather was still gloomy as Moore navigated the brightly-coloured Garda car through the morning traffic. It wasn't far to the solicitors' offices, but it still took twenty minutes to get there. Moore wondered why it was that the traffic always seemed to move much more slowly on grey, wet days than at any other time.

Inside the office, the woman at reception went through the usual rigmarole of calling internally to announce their presence.

"If you'd just like to take a seat, Inspector," she said, gesturing towards the rather boxy sofas and chairs dotted around the atrium.

Moore and Burke sat down as directed, but after five minutes observing the busy comings and goings, Burke said, "I've had enough of this. C'mon."

He got up and went back to the reception desk.

"Mr Mitchell?" he said, to remind the receptionist of their target.

"He's very busy this morning, Inspector, I'm trying to get him for you."

"So am I, Miss. What about if I just hopped over the turnstile there and went on up to his office? I know where it is."

"Just a moment, sir, I'll try him again," she said, reaching for the phone.

They didn't have to wait long. Mitchell came clip-clopping through the foyer at a brisk pace.

"Really, Inspector, have you people never heard of making an appointment? This is outrageous!"

"Our work doesn't run to a timetable, Mr Mitchell. Now, may we go to your office?"

"No, I'm afraid not. I have important clients in there. You'll have to make do with one of these small meeting rooms," the man said, determined to frustrate the Garda's efforts as much as possible.

"Very well. After you then," Burke said impatiently.

Chapter Twenty-Eight

"Mr Michell, it has come to our attention that one of the clients Jim Farrelly was working with has something of a reputation. Would you care to comment?" Burke said when they were all seated in a very small and airless room just off the main reception area.

Moore was sure that the room was used to intimidate potential interns who presented themselves for interview.

"I don't know what you're talking about. What client?"

"AMRAAL, Mr Mitchell. Does that help?"

"Inspector, we select our clients very carefully, I can assure you. They are all beyond reproach. So, whatever you think you may have heard is probably gossip put out by their competitors in an attempt to blacken their reputation."

Burke sighed impatiently, and Moore braced herself for what she felt was to come.

"Look, Mr Mitchell, please don't piss me about. I'm sure you know very well that there is talk that AMRAAL only want to set up here to avoid careful scrutiny of Trebutivan, and we know Jim Farrelly was aware of that fact. Did Jim Farrelly ever discuss that with you or anyone

else in the practice, and please resist your natural instinct to obfuscate, I'm not in the mood."

Mitchell said nothing for several moments. He just stared blankly at Burke who met his gaze with equal determination.

"Very well. Yes, he did in fact. He was concerned that the firm's reputation would be tainted if AMRAAL came unstuck. We would be honour-bound to represent them in any litigation, and it could get messy."

"What was decided?"

"The partners felt that in the light of the very substantial fee income AMRAAL were generating for us, we would continue to work with them, at least for the present."

"And what did Jim think of that?" Moore said.

"He wasn't happy. In fact, he never stopped banging on about it at partners' meetings. On one or two occasions it became quite heated. He was particularly bothered that his personal standing would be badly affected if he was seen to be involved with a rogue drug company. We have a few pharma clients, and he was concerned that they would leave us."

"I see. And just exactly how far had this lively debate progressed?" Burke said.

"I probably shouldn't tell you this, but Jim had threatened to leave Milligan Walker altogether. He would have had no problem joining another firm either here or in London. He was a well-respected advocate."

"And what would that have done for the firm, Mr Mitchell?" Moore said.

"It would have been, shall we say, a tad awkward, but we would have gotten over it, provided he kept quiet about AMRAAL," Mitchell said, but immediately regretted it. "I mean, it's all covered by confidentiality agreements, so there was no real risk to us."

"So, Mr Farrelly's passing is not entirely inconvenient then, given what you have told us?" Moore said.

"Now look here, Sergeant. I hope you're not suggesting that anyone here had anything to do with Jim's murder. That's beyond ridiculous! I won't have it!" Mitchell said, going bright red in the face.

"Of course I'm not suggesting anything of the kind. But someone saw him off, didn't they?" Burke said.

Burke decided to change the tempo a little. He produced copies of the coded notes from Farrelly's computer and showed them to Mitchell.

"Do these entries here in these notes mean anything to you, Mr Mitchell?"

Mitchell studied the papers, glad to have a change of topic.

"No, I can't say that they do. Where did you get them?"

"Hidden away on Farrelly's computer. Are you sure you don't recognize anything?" Burke said.

"Yes, certain. Now if that's all, I really must get back to my clients. They'll think I have abandoned them."

"Very well, Mr Mitchell. But we may need to come back at some stage. Oh, by the way, would Milligan Walker be handling a divorce on behalf of Farrelly's sister-in-law? Ward is the name."

"I very much doubt it," Mitchell said, smirking, pleased to be on safer ground. "We do very little in that area. It's too confrontational I'm afraid."

"Still, maybe you could check for us and let us know. They were family, so perhaps it's being processed here," Moore said.

"All right. I'll ask around," he said, standing up and ushering them out of the cramped space.

On the way back to Store Street, Moore asked her colleague, "You don't think there could be a connection to Farrelly's death lurking in there somewhere, do you, boss?"

"Who knows. Mitchell was very uneasy talking about it, that's for sure. And we still haven't established a clear motive for the murder, never mind the missus. Did we get any further with that insurance enquiry?"

"Oh, yes, we did. I should have told you. Jim Farrelly was insured under a death in service policy for seven times his annual pay, which would amount to around two million. There's a suicide clause in the policy, but apart from that, his missus would have been able to collect, not that she seemed to be in need of it."

"What about the Farrellys' wills?"

"As we thought. Everything is left one to another, but if either pre-decease, then the money goes to Sheila Ward. Jim has no siblings, and as we know there are no kids."

"Let's get this straight then. As things stand, Sheila Ward is set to inherit a couple of million, plus the value of the Farrellys' house, say another million, and whatever cash they have in the bank. Now there's a motive if ever I saw one," Burke said.

"Well, inheritance tax would gobble up about a third of that lot, but there would still be a right haul left. But surely you don't think Sheila Ward killed her sister?" Moore said.

"Why not? Two birds with one stone, if you see what I mean. With Brenda out of the way, she would have been able to be with Jim, and then there's the money."

"Hmm... maybe we should look a bit more closely at the woman, but your scenario rules out her having anything to do with Jim's demise."

"Yes, I know. It gets us back to the point where we may be looking at two entirely separate crimes, boss."

"Jesus! Just what we need!"

* * *

As the day progressed, information began to filter through to the detectives. The first morsel to land was Sheila Ward's bank account information. They could see where she was in receipt of a sizeable sum regularly from her husband, but those payments had ceased some four months before the murders, and Sheila Ward was now almost broke.

Next to arrive were the checks they had been making on the four air hostesses and the flight crew. These made for interesting reading. The senior stewardess, Marta, was loaded. She had a total of three bank accounts, and each had a very significant credit balance. Deposits of a couple of thousand euro in cash were made each week using automated machines in various locations, including Dublin Airport.

The other three girls had more modest funds, but they were by no means poor, and there was obviously some source of funds other than their pay from the airline going into their accounts.

Then information concerning Andrea Bergin came in from the Stockholm police. It described the woman as a 'person of interest' and invited the investigator to call an Inspector Lundqvist in the Stockholm police for more information.

As they pored over the documents, Moore said to her boss, "Do you think it would be better if I contacted Lundqvist, given the situation with Andrea Bergin?"

"And what situation would that be, Sergeant?" Burke said sourly.

Moore had the good sense not to reply.

After a minute or so, Burke responded, "Maybe you're right. Give him a shout, will you? And, Fiona, he doesn't need to know everything, OK?"

"Yes, boss, of course."

Chapter Twenty-Nine

Dónal Lawler was waiting for information to come back from forensics about the microchips that had been found in the device fitted to Brenda Ward's car that had caused her death. As he sat at his desk in the open plan, he doodled with the notes that had been found hidden on Jim Farrelly's laptop.

"OK," he said to himself, "the second set of numbers look like dates." Then he went to the printout of Farrelly's flights that they had received from European Airways, and matched the dates in the notes to days when Farrelly was travelling between the UK and Ireland. He also noticed that the flight numbers matched the first set of digits.

"Ah, so that's it. Something going on related to these flights. But what on earth does the rest of it mean?" he said, still muttering to himself.

He called Amy Sutton over, and asked her to have a look.

"These here seem to be dates and flight numbers, Amy, but I'm damned if I can figure out what the rest of it means. If only we could ask him," Lawler said.

Sutton looked at the pages for a few minutes.

"I don't know, Dónal, it could be anything. But maybe there's a way to find out."

"Oh. And what's that?"

"Couldn't one of us travel on that flight like Farrelly did and closely observe what's going on. If he could spot something, then so could we. Do you think the boss would go for it?" Sutton said.

"Cripes! I dunno. A bit dodgy, isn't it. And we'd have to use someone that the flight crew hadn't met, obviously," Lawler said.

"That shouldn't be a problem. I bet there are lots of cops that would look forward to a day out in London paid for by the taxpayer!"

"I guess you're right. Do you want to suggest it to Sergeant Moore?" Lawler said.

"Yes, OK. I'll catch her later."

When Amy Sutton had gone back to her own desk, Lawler put the notes with the numbers away. He was getting impatient, so he picked up the phone and called Daniel in forensics.

"Hi, Daniel, it's Dónal Lawler. Just wondering if you have any further information on that gizmo that was fitted to Mrs Farrelly's car?"

"Hi, Dónal. Yes, I have as it happens. It just came in this morning. The chips are made by a company called Nanotec. They specialize in control chips for all sorts of things like air-conditioners, freezers, and so on. I was able to retrieve a batch number form the ones we got from the car. All of the chips have to be uniquely identified down to the batch number for quality control reasons, you see."

"Yes, Daniel, fascinating. Can we get to the point?"

"OK, take it easy. This batch was sold to a wholesaler in Germany. They deal with the end customers. Nanotec just make the things."

"Right. Well, have you contacted the German outfit?"

"Yes, of course. It was a bit tricky, because the person they put me on to didn't have very good English, and my

German stops at 'guten Tag'. But I eventually managed to get my request across to her."

"Jesus, Daniel, and…?"

"Oh, they have to get back to me. They say those particular Nanotec chips are very popular. The sell loads of them all over, but they should be able to trace the batch number and where it went."

"OK. Well, let me know as soon as you have any word. This could be crucial to our investigation. Thanks, bye."

* * *

Fiona Moore didn't get hold of Inspector Lundqvist at the first attempt, but she did establish that Lundqvist was a woman. It didn't take long for her to call Moore back.

"Hello, Sergeant, this is Inspector Klara Lundqvist from the Stockholm police. How can I help you?"

"Hello, Inspector. Thanks for calling me back. I'm part of a team investigating a double murder here in Ireland. It's a nasty business I'm afraid. During our enquiries a name has come up that we think you might know something about. It's Andrea Bergin, does that mean anything to you?"

"Hold on a moment until I consult the database, Sergeant," Lundqvist said.

Moore could hear the clicking of the keyboard at the far end of the call and after a few moments, Lundqvist started talking again.

"Yes, I have the information here now. Andrea Bergin works as a pilot with one of those low-cost airlines. The address I have here is in Sollentuna, is that the one?"

"Yes, that's her. What have you got on her?"

"The file is rather long, I'm afraid. She hasn't been charged with anything, at least not here, but she is known to be somehow connected to the drugs trade. She lived with a guy in Stockholm for a couple of years and he was caught going through Manchester Airport with half a kilo of cocaine concealed about his person. He got ten years."

"And why have you been monitoring her, Inspector?"

"It's largely routine, but when her boyfriend was caught, we looked into her quite thoroughly, and found that she seems to have an awful lot of money for a co-pilot. But she is clever. We haven't been able to pin anything on her, but I'd swear she is still involved in drugs. Several of her close associates have connections to the drug trade too. May I ask what your interest is?"

Moore went on to explain about Jim Farrelly's death, but emphasized that they had no reason to connect Andrea Bergin to it directly, they were just looking into the full crew on the flight in question.

"That's interesting, because there was a somewhat similar case about eight months ago. It didn't involve a passenger, but there was a gate agent at Sturup, that's the airport for Malmö, who was poisoned in the same way as you describe. It turned out he was a small-time distributor of cocaine."

"Do you think there could be a connection, Inspector?" Moore said.

"Call me Klara, Sergeant. What's your first name?"

"Oh, OK. I'm Fiona."

"Look, Fiona, I can't say too much more about this just now. But our drugs police think there may be quite a big operation centred around airports and aviation that is being run out of Russia. They are finding it very difficult to get any good information, and their usual informants are saying nothing out of fear. They don't want to meddle too much with the people at the end of the chain. They want to go after the big guns, so they are being very discreet, and I'd appreciate it if the Garda keep this low key too."

"That's not up to me, I'm afraid, Klara, but I'll pass your request on up the line. But we do have a murder to solve here."

"Yes, I understand. But it would be a shame if the whole thing was blown wide open because of it. This could be very big."

"OK, well I'll do what I can. Thanks for the information in any case."

"You're welcome, bye."

When Moore hung up from speaking to the Swedish policewoman, she reflected on the conversation.

"God, I'm not looking forward to telling the boss about this! He'll probably have me transferred to the Aran Islands!" she said to herself.

Chapter Thirty

It was a dull, miserable Friday morning when Detective Garda Louise Grainger arrived by taxi outside Terminal 1 at Dublin Airport. They had bought her a ticket out on the early morning European Airways flight to Gatwick and back later that day on the last flight for a modest €39.99, and the transaction had been carried out in Grainger's personal capacity so as not to arouse any suspicion should anyone be observing. Grainger had managed to wheedle a further £100 in sterling from the Gardaí to cover her train ticket to London Victoria, her lunch, dinner and incidental expenses for the day. She was looking forward to the trip, and had been well briefed on what to look out for.

Louise Grainger was a good-looking woman, with long chestnut hair, green eyes, an oval face with high cheekbones, and an attractive figure. She was five feet, eight inches tall, and fetched some admiring glances as she made her way through the airport, down the endless corridors to the departure gate.

The flight to England was very straightforward. The plane was nearly full, and Grainger noted the names of the cabin attendants. There were two females and two males. The senior cabin attendant was called Marta, assisted by

Sadie, Viktor and Benjamin. As expected, most of the passengers ordered a hot drink, and several took breakfast rolls from the crew as the aircraft plied its way across the Irish Sea, past Strumble Head, along the south coast of England, finally turning in to land smoothly on Gatwick's main runway, designated 08R.

During the flight, Grainger was seated beside a rather portly businessman who busied himself with papers that he was working on, no doubt in preparation for some meetings or other that he would attend later in the City. Conversation with her neighbour was limited to short greetings, although he did offer to get Grainger's handbag down from the overhead bin when they arrived at their destination.

Louise Grainger avoided the Gatwick Express on the basis that it was very costly, and took the regular train into Victoria that stopped at two stations along the way: East Croydon and Clapham Junction.

Once at Victoria, Grainger took to the underground and travelled to Oxford Circus with some serious shopping, or at least some extensive browsing, in mind. She spent the morning going up and down Oxford Street, looking at clothes, shoes, handbags and souvenirs, and by lunchtime was beginning to feel the early start and the traipsing around making her weary, so she found a cosy pub on Berners Street, and settled down to a bowl of homemade soup and a chicken sandwich.

By five o'clock it was time to get back to Victoria for the journey south to the airport. Again, Grainger avoided the Gatwick Express, and took the slow train, though in truth, it was only marginally slower and a hell of a lot cheaper. She opted for a Portsmouth train that went through Gatwick, and then on to Three Bridges, Christs Hospital, Arundel, and eventually into Portsmouth.

The homebound flight was very different to the early morning service from Dublin. Gatwick was busy, and it took a good while to get through security where Grainger was photographed and thoroughly scanned, with her handbag being more or less turned out for inspection. The shopping bags she had acquired during the day were also well scrutinized, and the bottle of water she was keeping to remain hydrated was taken from her and binned.

After what seemed like an age, and some very unnecessary procedures, she finally arrived at the departure gate just as the inbound plane was docking. Grainger had opted for an aisle seat a little over halfway down the cabin, so she could observe both sets of cabin crew going about their busy service. As she boarded through the forward passenger door, she noticed that Marta, the senior cabin attendant, was in the cockpit talking to the flight crew.

There was quite a mixture of passengers on board. The obligatory hen party of ten girls all well-oiled before they set off, dressed in what they thought were amusing T-shirts and very short skirts; businessmen and women; some younger men who may have been students; and a few genuine tourists who from their accents could be traced to North America.

Grainger was seated beside two young men who apparently didn't know each other. When they had taken their seats, the nearest one engaged her in conversation, asking her if she had been shopping in London and if she had managed to get everything that she wanted. He told her he was a trainee accountant who had emigrated to London following university and went home as often as he could to see his family and friends in Ireland.

Before take-off, once the cabin door had been closed, the public address system crackled into life.

"Good evening, ladies and gentlemen," a woman's voice said, "this is your captain Andrea Bergin from the flight deck. We will be on our way in just a few moments. Weather on route is good this evening, and we expect to be in Dublin on time at nine-fifteen. I will be flying you across, ably assisted by Captain Piotr Kaan. Marta and her crew will look after you in the cabin, and can I ask you to ensure that your seat belts are fastened and mobile devices switched off for take-off. Thank you for choosing European Airways for your flight this evening. I'll speak to you again before we land in Dublin."

Grainger noted that it was the same crew that had worked the morning flight, except that this time, Marta and Viktor were providing service in the aft section of the cabin. After roughly twenty minutes, the trolley arrived at Grainger's seat row, and the two men seated beside her ordered beers.

"Is there anything else at all I can get you?" Marta said, leaning over Louise Grainger to deliver the drinks.

The young man seated at the window took a €50 note which was folded up so that it was very small from his trouser pocket and slipped it to Marta. She looked up and down the aisle to see if anyone was watching, and then deftly passed the man something small, taking the cash and putting it in her tunic pocket. She then moved quickly on to the next row. Grainger saw the transaction, which was executed in a very slick and well-practiced fashion, but only because she was looking out for it. She doubted if anyone else saw what was going on, so covert was the transfer. The guy in the middle seat didn't even appear to have seen what had taken place.

Grainger pretended that nothing had happened and the rest of the flight went past quickly and without further incident. When they were about ten minutes out from Dublin, the captain came back on the loudspeakers.

"Ladies and gentlemen, we will be landing in Dublin in ten minutes. After landing, please remain seated until the Fasten Seat Belt sign has been extinguished. Once again, thank you for flying with us tonight, and have a safe onward journey."

Back in Dublin, Louise Grainger got a taxi to her apartment in Drumcondra, pleased with her day's work. When she had settled in, and changed into a comfy dressing gown and prepared a cup of tea, she called Fiona Moore.

"Hi, Sarge, I'm back."

"Hello, Louise. How did it go?"

"Exhausting. That's one hell of a long day. But I got what we need, I think." She explained what had happened.

"Really! Oh, that's great, Louise. Can you follow up with European Airways and get the name and details of the customer who bought the stuff. We may need that later."

"Yes, sure, see you then."

Moore then called Burke.

"Are you on your own, boss?" she asked, not sure whether Burke had Andrea Bergin with him or not.

"Yes, I made some excuse about work for this weekend so as not to complicate matters further," Burke said.

"Probably just as well," Moore said and went on to tell him what Louise Grainger had told her about the Gatwick–Dublin flight.

"Fuck it!" he said, followed by a short silence.

"OK, well can you get Dónal and Amy in as well. This gives us something concrete to go on, at least. Is there anything else?"

"No, boss. But can I ask, what are you going to tell the Super?"

"I don't know, Fiona. I haven't figured it out yet. But I'll think of something, don't worry. Goodnight."

When the call was ended, Moore sent a WhatsApp message to Dónal Lawler and Amy Sutton requesting their attendance in the Garda station the following morning. She waited until the two tick marks had gone blue signifying that they had received and read the message.

Chapter Thirty-One

The detectives' floor at Store Street was sparsely populated on the Saturday morning when the team arrived carrying takeaway coffees in cardboard cups. Burke got them all together in the open plan, and addressed the group.

"Right, folks, it looks like you were right, Dónal, this may in fact be two separate cases of murder. Unusual, I grant you, but that's the way the evidence is pointing at the moment in any case. So, we need to divide and conquer, as it were. But firstly, have we any more information in on any of the suspects?"

Fiona Moore relayed the information that she had received from Klara Lundqvist, keeping a close eye on her boss for a reaction, but he remained poker-faced.

"Hmm… OK, that's interesting. When I was over there, something a bit odd happened too. Andrea left the apartment for an hour or so on the Sunday morning, and later when I was getting my bag from the boot of her car, I saw a strange-looking package partly concealed in the boot. It could easily have been drugs. It was wrapped around with brown parcel tape just like the packs we usually come across."

"So, what's the plan, boss?" Amy Sutton asked.

"I want to split us up into two teams. Fiona, can you work with Dónal here? I'll take Amy and we'll keep going on Mrs Farrelly's murder. We need to find out more about this Ward chap, and see if we can't tie the device that was found in her car back to him, if that's what happened. And there's something else. It could easily be that Sheila Ward's life is in danger. If Ward wants to get his hands on the Farrelly money pronto, he may have plans to bump her off as well to speed things up a bit. So, Amy, can you drive out to her place and get her to take precautions. I think she should hire a different car, and maybe go and stay with friends or something. I'm afraid you will have to press home the seriousness of her position, but try not to scare the living daylights out of her. OK?"

"Yes, sure, boss."

"I'm going to dig around in Ward's business affairs a bit and see if there's anything there. Then, I think we should pay him another visit at his place of work."

"What else do you want us to do?" Fiona Moore said.

"We have almost a week before that flight crew will be back in Dublin. It seems they all stay together and work three Gatwick flights on a Friday. I'd like us to have our ducks in a row by then. Maybe you could coordinate with the Swedish police and have Bergin's apartment and car searched while she's flying around the place. She'll probably be staying overnight in Gatwick for the week anyway, so the coast should be clear for them to have a nosey around. If they are selling drugs onboard those flights, I want to arrest them here. I don't want Lundqvist getting all the glory! Start with that Marta girl. Get everything you can on her. Dig deep. She may have slipped up before. Then see what you can find out about Andrea Bergin's old boyfriend. There should be records on him somewhere in the system. We will have daily catch-up meetings here to make sure we're getting somewhere with it all. OK, everyone?"

"Yes, sir," they all said in unison.

"Right. Let's get off and enjoy what's left of the weekend, except you, Amy. You need to go and see Sheila Ward as soon as possible. Oh, before we go, how tight is the information Louise Grainger got on her day trip?"

"I've spoken to her, boss. She made contemporaneous notes and she has the name and contact details for the bloke that bought the snow from the hostess, and she thinks he'd probably give evidence discreetly rather than have his habit exposed. Apparently, he works for one of the big accountancy firms here in Dublin," Moore said.

"Snow?" Burke said.

"Sorry, cocaine, sir. It's a slang term for the stuff," Moore said blushing slightly.

"Oh, right. God, I'll never catch up with all this jargon."

* * *

Amy Sutton phoned ahead to make sure that Sheila Ward was at home before driving out to Kinsealy to see the woman. When she got to the house, Mrs Ward spotted her car advancing up the drive, and was standing at the open front door when Sutton approached.

"Good morning, Mrs Ward. Sorry to bother you, but I wonder if we could have a word?"

"Yes, of course. Come in. I'm just making some coffee. Would you like a cup?"

"Thanks, that would be lovely," Sutton said.

When they were seated at the kitchen table, Sheila Ward asked, "So, what's all this about, Detective?"

"I'm sorry, Mrs Ward, but there's no easy way to say this, but we think there is a slight chance your life might be in danger."

Sheila Ward nearly choked on a mouthful of her drink, and spluttered and coughed while reaching for a tissue to mop up the mess. When she had recovered somewhat, she said, "How do you mean? That sounds a bit unlikely, don't you think?"

"Yes, I agree. But while the investigation into Brenda's death is ongoing, we can't rule anything out, and it's much better to be safe than sorry, don't you think?"

"But who do you think might wish me harm?" Ward said.

"I'm not at liberty to discuss that at this point, Sheila, but we have credible information that the person or persons that killed your sister may want you out of the way too. That's all I can say for the present. Now it has been suggested that you go and stay with a friend for a few days while we get to the bottom of this, and we'd like you not to drive your regular car too. Can you hire something?"

Sheila Ward remained silent for a few minutes while she processed what she had been told.

"You think it's Peter, don't you?" she said.

"Sorry?"

"You think Peter killed Brenda, don't you?"

"As I said, Sheila, we're not–"

Sheila Ward spoke across Amy Sutton.

"That's completely ridiculous. I know we are separated, but there is no way in heaven that my ex-husband would be involved in such things. And as for bumping me off, well, that's just outrageous! You have this all wrong, I promise you."

"We aren't accusing anyone at this point in time, Sheila, but we are very keen that you take the precautions that I have outlined. What harm can it do to be careful, after all?"

"As I said, I think you are being ridiculous, but I'll do as you ask, but only for a few days."

"Thank you. I'm sorry if it's inconvenient, but we would feel happier knowing that you are safe."

"All right, but promise me you will contact me as soon as it's OK to return here. I like my home, and my car for that matter. I don't want to be away for long."

"Yes, of course, and thanks for your cooperation."

Amy Sutton got up from the table having drained her coffee cup, and said goodbye to Sheila Ward. Before she left, she made sure that she had the woman's mobile phone number, and the address of where she would be for the next few days. She left Mrs Ward to make the arrangements for a hire car as had been agreed.

Sheila Ward stood in the doorway of her house and watched Sutton get into her car and drive away. When the detective had exited the premises, and the gates had closed behind her, Ward went back into the kitchen and picked up her mobile phone. She dialled a number and waited for it to answer.

"Hi, it's me," she said to the person who answered with the single word 'yes'.

"Hi, what's up?"

"I've just had a visit from the police," she said and went on to relate what Amy Sutton had said to her.

"We need to be very careful. It looks like they smell a rat. Have you got things covered from your end?"

"Yes, well, as far as I can in any case. I think we're OK. Just keep your nerve. I guess I should expect a visit then."

"Yes, I'd say so. Be careful, love."

"You too." And the call ended.

Chapter Thirty-Two

Monday morning was busy at Store Street. Burke was probing the records of Power Electronic Devices. The company had filed accounts eight months earlier, and looked at that time to be in good shape. There were decent profits and a healthy turnover, even though the outfit was quite heavily indebted. Burke noted that there had been a sizeable write-down for research and development, a method often used by these sorts of companies to minimize exposure to tax.

He was about to call Power Electronic Devices' bank, when his desk phone rang.

"Hello, Inspector. It's Daniel here from forensics."

"Oh, hi, Daniel, what have you got?"

"I've been doing some more work on that gizmo we took from Brenda Farrelly's car. I had been concentrating on the printed circuit, but on Saturday I noticed something about the two little wires sticking out of it. They are insulated copper, but that's not unusual. What is unusual though is that they are of a very high specification. Firstly, they are tinned copper. That stuff is used in very high-end electronics. It's more heat resistant than the ordinary copper wire, and it's a better conductor too."

"I see. Anything else?"

"Yes, there is. This stuff is so specialized that there's a manufacturer's name and batch number printed along the outside of the red wire on the insulation. I haven't got the entire number, because there isn't enough of the wire, but there's quite a bit of it."

"Excellent. Have you been on to the manufacturer, Daniel?"

"I have put in a call. They're in Germany. They said they would call me back this afternoon."

"Great. Well, let me know as soon as you can. That's good work, Daniel. Thanks."

"No problem, sir."

Burke then called the National Bank in Naas where Power Electronic Devices had their account. After a bit of obfuscation, he got through to Keith Barton, the manager. Burke explained that he was doing some background research on the company in connection with a case they were working on, but gave no details to the banker.

"I was just wondering if you could tell me a little about PED's accounts – if they are healthy and so on?"

"Inspector, may I call you back on your switchboard's number? You could be just anyone after all," Barton said.

"Yes, of course, it's 607…"

"No, don't tell me. I'll look it up in the phone book, if you don't mind."

"Oh, yes, of course. Sorry. I'll await your call."

Three minutes later, Burke's phone rang.

"Inspector, it's Barton here from the National Bank in Naas."

"Ah, yes, Mr Barton, thanks for calling back. As you can see, I'm the real thing!"

"Yes, quite. Now, about Power Electronic Devices. I've been concerned about their account for some months. They are right up against their overdraft limit, in fact they are in excess of it more or less all the time, and last month we had to have discussions with Peter Ward about paying their staff. Head office isn't happy, and we may have to foreclose, even though that would make us very unpopular in the town. I'm trying to find a solution, but Ward is adamant that he'll be able to sort it out very shortly. I really hope so."

"What sort of money are we talking about, Mr Barton?"

"It's no secret if you've seen his accounts. They have an overdraft of €250,000, and a term loan of another €100,000 that has almost a year to run."

"How come they are in such bad shape? Last year's accounts look very healthy," Burke said.

"It seems they have had to make some very large pay-outs to two of their customers over faulty merchandise. I don't know the details, but apparently a few of their control units went rogue and some equipment overheated and was badly damaged. The customer was threatening litigation, so they settled, but it was very costly."

"I see. Will they survive?"

"I'm not sure. Ward is talking about a big cash injection that he is lining up, but he hasn't provided any details. But that's what most entrepreneurs do when they get into a tight spot."

"How long has he got?" Burke said.

"I'd say between two and three months. Then if things don't improve, we'll have to call it in. It would be a pity if it comes to that. He has quite a few from the town employed, and it won't do us any good if we close him down. But head office doesn't care about that. They just want to see their cash back."

"OK. Well, thanks for the information, Mr Barton. And I'll keep your name out if it if this develops at all."

"Thanks, Inspector, much appreciated."

When he had finished the call, Burke summoned Amy Sutton.

"C'mon, Amy, get your coat, we're going for a drive in the country," he said.

Sutton didn't know what the inspector was up to, but she knew better than to challenge him. The man had a reputation for being quite brusque with the junior officers, but still, Amy was looking forward to being his bagman for a while and was prepared to tolerate his occasional intemperate mood.

When they were seated in Burke's car and driving up along the canal, Amy sensed that his humour was a bit better, and she ventured, "Where are we off to, sir?"

"Naas, Amy. I need to speak to Peter Ward. Forensics have come up with some useful little nuggets that we need to check out. When we get there, I'll lead, but you keep your eyes and ears open and try not to miss anything."

"Right. I'll do my best."

She felt a little like a rather dim schoolgirl that had just been told off by the teacher, but she swallowed it all the same. However, she was determined to prove that she could add value to the situation, despite her boss's obvious misgivings.

On arrival, the two detectives were ushered into Peter Ward's office where the man was seated behind his desk.

"Good morning, Inspector. Please, take a seat. Can I arrange some coffee for you both?" Ward said.

"No thanks, Mr Ward, we won't keep you long. I just have a few questions for clarification from you. Can I ask where you get the microprocessors that go into the temperature control units you manufacture here?"

"Gracious, you do believe in getting straight to the point, don't you, Inspector. We use various suppliers, but most of them come from a distributor in Belgium. Why do you ask?"

"Well, you see, Mr Ward, I have a little problem. We found a device with some circuitry in it that almost certainly caused Brenda's death. We examined it very carefully, and from what we can see the microchips in it are the same ones that are supplied to you here for use in your manufacturing. How do you explain that?" Burke said.

"So? We are not the exclusive user of those things. They're probably bashed out in China by the hundreds, and temperature control circuits go into loads of things from domestic freezers to jet engines, and everything in between. You're not suggesting I had anything to do with poor Brenda's accident, are you?"

"Mr Ward, I'm just a humble policeman, trying to follow a trail of evidence, such as it is, to solve two very puzzling killings. What can you tell me about the financial health of your business, Mr Ward?"

Before Ward could answer, Amy Sutton intervened.

"I'm sorry, sir, I'm not feeling very well. Would you mind if I went outside and got some fresh air?"

The two men looked at Amy, and Burke said, "No, of course. Off you go. I'll see you downstairs in a few minutes."

Amy got up and left the room.

"You were about to tell me about your company's finances, Mr Ward," Burke said.

"Was I? Well, presumably you know something, or you wouldn't have asked. PED is going through a bit of a rough patch just now. It's nothing serious. We've had issues in the past and managed to come through, so I'm confident that this will be no different."

"What's the problem?"

"I really don't want to go into the details, Inspector, it's very sensitive commercially. But I'm confident that it will all work out."

"What can you tell me about the Farrellys' wills, Mr Ward?"

"How do you mean?"

"Well, they were both well off, and Jim Farrelly's life insurance policy will yield a pretty penny. Where do you think that money will end up now that Brenda is dead?"

"I really haven't a clue. I have more to be doing than digging into the wills of my ex-wife's relatives, I can assure you. It's got nothing whatever to do with me."

"But Sheila isn't exactly your ex-wife, is she?"

"Of course she is. You know we are no longer together."

"But not actually divorced, or legally separated, isn't that right?"

"So what? We are going through the process. As you may know, it's a long and expensive procedure in Ireland. And there's no reason to hurry it up. It's not as if I'm waiting to marry someone else or anything."

"Oh, yes, Mr Ward, I do know all about it. I've been there myself."

Ward was quiet for a minute. Burke waited for what he knew was coming.

"Look, Inspector, you seem to have got it into your head that I may be someway involved in all of this. Well, you're quite wrong. I have no interest in the Farrellys or their money. I don't even know what they were worth. And I resent you coming here fishing for some morsel of evidence to tie my company into Brenda's accident that simply doesn't exist. Now if you don't mind, I have things to do. And if you want to speak to me again about any of this, I will want to have a solicitor present. Do you understand?"

"Oh yes, Mr Ward, I understand perfectly. And if I may say so, I think that would be very wise."

Chapter Thirty-Three

When Burke was gone, Ward stood up and stared out the window at the end of his office that overlooked the car park. He watched as the two detectives got back into Burke's car. They chatted for a moment before the white reversing lights came on, and Burke backed out of the space, changed gears, and drove off briskly.

Then he went to the phone.

"Hi. It's me. Listen, I've just had that nosey copper here again. I think he was just fishing, but I don't like it. It might be a good idea if you took off for a few days. What do you think?"

"Hmm... maybe. They were around here earlier giving me the same advice," Sheila Ward said.

"Oh, really? So it won't spook them if you vanish for a while till things settle down. By the way, how's the other business coming along?"

"Well, I think I've got hold of Brenda's current account. I had to fill in loads of forms at the bank and produce a copy of the will, but they're going to release the funds pending probate as long as I indemnify them."

"That's terrific. You're a star, Sheila. That will see us right for this month's payroll at least. Look, I'd better go. Talk soon. OK?"

"Yes, OK, and I'll be careful. Love you."

"You too."

* * *

"Are you feeling better now, Amy?" Burke said as they joined the M7 just north of Naas.

Sutton didn't reply, but reached into her handbag and took something out and placed it on top of the dashboard. Burke glanced over at the item.

"What's that?"

"That, Inspector, is the tail end of a spool of insulated copper wire. And I'd bet next month's salary that it's the same kind that was used to wire up Brenda Farrelly's car."

"Christ, Amy! How did you get hold of that?"

"When I went walkabout, I found some bins around the back of the building. One of them was labelled 'electronic waste', so I had a root, and voilà. There's only about two turns of wire left on the little spool, but it should be enough for Daniel to get a match, or not, as the case may be."

"So, you weren't feeling unwell at all then?"

"No. Of course not. But you told me not to miss anything, sir."

Burke smiled broadly.

"Well done you, Amy!"

* * *

Fiona Moore was busy. They had a few days to set things up for Friday, when it was hoped they would be able to arrest the European Airways crew on various drug charges. But before they could do that, they needed more evidence.

The first thing she did was to get hold of Louise Grainger.

"Hi, Louise, it's Sergeant Moore here. I'd like you to contact that man you were sitting beside on the flight who bought the cocaine. We need him to make a statement. Tell him he's not in trouble, and we won't be prosecuting him or anything, but we need him to record how he purchased the drugs from the cabin attendant. Can you do that?"

"I'll try, Sergeant. I have his details. I got them from the airline. But he may not want to have anything to do with it," Grainger said.

"I'm sure you can persuade him, Louise. Use the fact that we know he is a user as leverage, and if he still won't cooperate, tell him we will have to inform his employer about his habit."

"Crikey! Would you really do that, Sergeant? He seemed like a nice bloke."

"No, I wouldn't, Louise, but he doesn't know that, does he?"

"No, I guess not. OK. I'll get in touch and let you know how it goes."

The next call Moore made was to Lundqvist in Stockholm. When she got speaking to the inspector, she outlined their plan for Friday.

"OK, so you are quite certain that this particular crew are selling drugs on board?" Lundqvist said.

"Yes, we are, in fact we have proof of it. So, we want to move in on them before they realize we are onto them. Is there any way you could search Bergin's apartment while she is staying in the UK?"

"I don't think so. We would need a warrant, and I haven't enough evidence to get one at this point. I tell you what, though. We could search her car. We don't need a warrant for that, and I'm sure it's parked at Arlanda in the staff car park. If it's not there it will be at her home address, but better if it's at the airport. It's easier to justify the search."

"That would be great, Klara. When do you think you could do that?"

"Maybe tomorrow. I'll see how we are fixed. I'll let you know what happens."

"Great, thanks."

When she had finished the call, Moore turned her attention to the cabin crew. They had done some background checking on the four, but it hadn't turned up much. The one she was most interested in was Marta, as they had evidence that she was actually dealing. Marta was Polish. Her home was on the outskirts of Gdansk where she lived with her family along with two siblings. She was obviously clever, given her degrees from Gdansk University, and her command of so many languages. But Moore needed to know more.

Having asked around if any of her colleagues had any contacts in the Polish police, and drawn a blank, Moore decided there was nothing for it. She would have to make a cold call to Gdansk herself and see if she could find out anything more.

It took several hours of continuous effort before she was able to get through to anyone who was able, or indeed willing, to help her. Eventually she got speaking to an Inspector Nowak, who had excellent English, and a friendly disposition.

"Ah, good day, Sergeant. Nice to hear someone from Dublin. My daughter lives there in somewhere called Smithfield. Do you know it?"

"Yes, of course, it's not far from here," Moore said, hoping the man wouldn't want to know anything more about the place which had a decidedly mixed reputation. She pressed on with her enquiry before he could question her further.

"I'm trying to get information on a Marta Dudek. She lived in Gdansk and attended the university there, but now she works for an airline and is based in Gatwick in the United Kingdom."

"Just a moment, I'll see if we have anything in our system for her. Do you have an address in Gdansk?"

"No, I'm sorry, I don't. But I have her date of birth if that helps?"

"Yes, please," Nowak said.

"It's 20 March 1993."

Moore could hear the tapping of a computer keyboard as Nowak searched for information on the girl.

"OK, well we have a file. But I can't access it on this system, Sergeant. Can you give me a few hours to dig a little bit deeper? I'll have to go and ask a colleague to give me access."

"Yes, of course. I'm sorry for the trouble," Moore said, impressed with the lengths Nowak was prepared to go to for her.

"It's no trouble, just a nuisance that I can't access it from my desk. Some of our computer systems need updating."

"Yes, I know what you mean. So do ours."

Nowak laughed briefly.

"I imagine it's the same all over, Sergeant. Anyway, give me your contact details and I'll get back to you as soon as I can."

Moore did the necessary and thanked the man for his help.

Chapter Thirty-Four

The week was passing slowly. The detectives were assembling such evidence as they could get their hands on, and preparing for Friday when they hoped to have enough to arrest several members of the flight crew.

Garda Louise Grainger had collected the statement from the airline passenger that had bought the drugs on the flight back from Gatwick. He had been reluctant at first to get involved, not really believing Grainger that the Gardaí wouldn't prosecute him for his habit. But the young Garda persisted, and cajoled, and eventually she obtained what she needed. There was now no way that Marta could wriggle out of her lucrative side-line.

It was Wednesday when Amy Sutton came into Burke's office.

"Got a minute, boss?"

"Yes, sure, Amy, come in, grab a seat. What's up?"

"I think we may have just got a lucky break. I went back out to the site of Mrs Farrelly's car crash. You know the way you always say 'let the scene speak to you'?"

"Yes, and?"

"There's a tall wooden electrical pole at the side of the road a little way back from the bridge. I spotted a funny-looking black box positioned high up on it, and got curious."

"Yes, yes, OK. Get to the punch line, Amy," Burke said.

"Well, it turns out Fingal County Council have been recording traffic at that particular spot for a month or so. They are thinking about re-aligning the road to make it safer, and want to see what the traffic patterns are. It seems they do this quite a lot at busy intersections and so on," Sutton said.

"Interesting. So did you get anything useful?"

"Yes, I did as it happens. When I finally tracked down the contractors that Fingal have hired to do the recording – it wasn't easy, I can tell you – I got hold of the film from the day of the crash. You'll never guess what came up."

"Good God, Amy, get on with it. I'm growing old here."

"Sorry, boss. Following not too far behind Mrs Farrelly's car was none other than Peter Ward in his fancy machine. And when Brenda Farrelly had done her somersault act, he did a three-point turn and went back the way he had come."

"Cripes! Nice one. But listen, I want this tied up really tight. I think we have enough to lift Ward at this stage, but he's a smart cookie. I don't want him to wriggle out from under on some technicality. So, make sure it's all properly obtained and recorded. And don't say anything to anyone outside for the moment. I want to think out how best to handle this now. Arrange to have the whole team here tomorrow at nine o'clock and we'll brainstorm a plan."

* * *

It was late in the afternoon when Fiona Moore's phone rang.

"Moore," she said.

"Hello, Sergeant, this is Klara Lundqvist from Stockholm. I have some news for you."

"Oh, hello, Klara. What's that then?"

"We did as you suggested. We found Bergin's car out at Arlanda, as we expected. We gave it a good going-over, and found quite an amount of cocaine residue in the boot. We also found a small box of little plastic bags under the passenger's seat. Just like the ones that are used to pack a single dose of the drug. So, it looks as if she is definitely involved, or should I say, up to her neck in it."

"That's fantastic, Klara. Thank you so much. I'm not sure how this works now. How can we use this new information as evidence to arrest her?"

"That's not a problem. I'll have the paperwork drawn up here, and we can issue a European Arrest Warrant that you can execute over there. Once you have her in custody, we are going to move on several others that we are aware of too. So, keep in touch as soon as you have her. She may provide evidence we can use against some of the rest of them."

"Do you think you will be able to get at the people behind the whole thing?"

"Fiona, those people are sunbathing on thirty-metre yachts in the Caribbean completely oblivious to what is going on here. We won't get them, but we may be able to disrupt their operation for a while, seize some of their assets, lift some of the middlemen. We'll never get on top of the drugs trade, but that doesn't mean we won't keep trying."

"I know. I agree. Anyway, I'd better keep going, Klara. Thanks for your help," Moore said.

* * *

"OK, everyone, listen up," Burke said at nine o'clock the following morning when the team had all arrived.

"First, Mr Peter Ward. Thanks to Amy here, we have enough evidence to bring Ward in. But I don't want to do that yet."

Moore looked very surprised by her boss's statement.

"But why ever not, boss? As you say, we have enough on him to charge him," she said.

"Yes, but I am starting to think that Sheila Ward and her husband set this whole thing up. And I fancy we could get the wife to talk more easily than Peter. You know the technique. We'll bring her in. Tell her about the evidence we have on her husband and what that means, and put her under some real pressure. My bet is she'll crack. What do you think?" Burke said.

"I hope it doesn't backfire, boss," Moore said.

"It won't. Trust me."

Moore said nothing.

"When we've finished here, you and I will go out to where Mrs Ward is staying and bring her in. OK, Sergeant?"

"Yes, of course," Moore said, hoping her boss's plan would work.

"Right, now on to Friday night. We are going to need a bunch of uniforms to ensure we get both Marta and her accomplice. Have we anything back from the Polish police about the stewardess, Fiona?"

"Yes, Inspector Nowak got back to me this morning. Marta Dudek was done for possession a few years ago. It was just personal use, so she got a fine and a few months' probation. She hasn't any further convictions, but while she was on probation, she was observed mixing with some rather unsavoury characters. They could never get anything on her, and they lost interest when she moved away. But Klara Lundqvist says she thinks they are part of quite an extensive gang selling a right lot of drugs onboard various flights, and to aircraft and airport workers. The Swedish police are going to move on some of them when we have our two in custody."

"OK, so will you liaise with the Airport Police to set things up. I want our men togged out in European Airways high-vis vests and milling around the inbound plane from Gatwick. When the passengers have deplaned, you and I will go on board and arrest Bergin and Dudek. Then you can call Lundqvist and get her moving before the news breaks."

"Do you want to alert the airline, boss?" Moore asked.

"God, no. The fewer people that know what's going on, the better. And that goes for around here too. If there's any sort of a leak, the operation will be blown. We will hold a briefing with all concerned and we'll go early on Friday. I'd like to intercept them on their first flight into Dublin. That way if they are dealing, they'll have a good lot of cocaine stashed somewhere," Burke said.

"But how do you think this can be connected to Jim Farrelly's murder, boss?" Dónal Lawler asked.

"Patience, dear man, patience. All will be revealed."

Chapter Thirty-Five

Burke and Moore drove out to where Sheila Ward was staying, having phoned ahead to ensure that she would be in. The woman tried to get some information from the detectives as to what they wanted her for, but they said that they just needed to clarify one or two things.

When they got to the house, Sheila Ward opened the door and invited the two Gardaí in.

"We won't come in, Mrs Ward, but we'd like you to accompany us to Store Street station please."

"Oh, what's all this about?" Ward said.

"We just need to ask you a few more questions, and clarify some of the things you have told us previously. And I'd like you to give me your mobile phone, please," Burke said.

"I see. Should I have a solicitor present?"

"That's up to you, Mrs Ward, but you're not actually under arrest, we just want you to help us with our enquiries."

"Very well. Let me just get my coat, then I'll be with you."

Burke nodded to Amy Sutton and the detective followed Sheila Ward into the house while she got her handbag from the kitchen and her coat from the hall.

When she got to the door, Burke asked her again for her phone.

"I'm not very happy about handing this over, Inspector. What are you going to do with it?"

"Nothing. I just would prefer if you didn't use it while we are driving back to town. If you need a solicitor, you can call one from the station."

Ward handed over the phone, but not before turning it off.

When they got back to Store Street, the woman was shown into one of the more comfortable rooms and asked if she would like any refreshment.

Moore and Burke went in and sat down opposite Sheila Ward.

"Mrs Ward, I'd just like to inform you that you are not at this time under arrest," Burke said. "You are at liberty to have a solicitor present if you wish. If you haven't got ready access to one, we can provide the duty solicitor for you, and you are of course free to leave at any time. Do you understand?"

"Yes, of course, I'm not an idiot, Inspector."

"So, do you want a solicitor then?"

"Not for now, no. I take it if I change my mind that won't be a problem?"

"Of course not. Right then, let's get started. Do you have any idea why you are here, Mrs Ward?"

"None at all. I have recently lost my sister in very tragic circumstances, and frankly, I think you are being very unfair bringing me here like a common criminal."

"That's what we wanted to talk to you about, Mrs Ward. As you know, we have discovered evidence to suggest that your sister, Brenda Farrelly, was murdered. A device was fitted to her car that caused it to accelerate out of control and crash into the bridge at high speed. Further analysis of the device in question indicates that it may be connected to your husband's firm, Power Electronic Devices. Do you know anything about that?"

"That's ridiculous! What analysis? Why would Peter want anything to do with Brenda's death?"

"The device in question contained microchip circuitry. The microchips are of the same type and brand as those used in Mr Ward's operation, and the wire used to connect the device to the cruise control mechanism in Mrs Farrelly's car is exactly the same type and from the same manufacturer as Mr Ward uses too. Rather a coincidence, don't you think?" Burke said.

"Well, maybe, but that's all it is. What possible reason would Peter have to kill my sister? I mean, he didn't even know her that well."

"Money," Moore said.

"How do you mean, money? What's that got to do with anything?"

"Well, the way I see it, you stand to inherit a very large sum of money from the death of the Farrellys. There's Brenda's own money, a considerable sum in its own right, and then there's Jim Farrelly's insurance pay-out which will run to a few million. And it all goes to you, isn't that right?" Burke said.

"Yes, I suppose so, but I hadn't really thought about that aspect of it. I've been too busy grieving for my poor dead sister."

"Mrs Ward, isn't it true that Peter Ward's business is in trouble for money? After all, he appears to have stopped paying you the monthly allowance that was agreed when you separated, and as far as we can establish, the business is close to bust. Were you aware of this?"

"Look, Inspector, Peter and I are separated. I have as little to do with him as I can manage, and as for his firm being broke, that's laughable. Do you know how much his contracts with those tech companies he supplies are worth?" Sheila Ward said.

"Were worth, Mrs Ward. He's lost most of those recently. Apparently, the temperature sensors he's making aren't as good as he thought they were," Moore said.

"Well, I don't know anything about that. I never did understand that business anyway. Now, if that's all, may I go please?"

"Not just yet, if you don't mind. But I'd like to take a rest break for about twenty minutes. Would you like a cup of tea of coffee, Mrs Ward?" Burke said.

"Yes please. Tea, no sugar and just a drop of milk."

* * *

Outside the interview room, Burke handed Sheila Ward's phone to Moore.

"Take this thing upstairs and see what you can get from it. I want to check something else out. How do you think it's going?"

"Not well. She's going to walk in a few minutes, and probably tip Ward off. Then we'll be rightly snookered!"

"We'll see."

* * *

Twenty minutes later Burke and Moore met up again outside the interview room.

"Well, anything?" Burke said.

"Bingo!" Moore said, waving Sheila Ward's phone in her hand.

"OK, good. We'd better get back in there. You lead with whatever you've got, OK?"

"Sure," Moore said, relishing the thought.

Sheila Ward was looking confident as they re-entered the room. She had just about finished the tea that she had been given, and looked if she was ready to depart.

"Mrs Ward, I'd like you to explain some of these messages that we found on your phone between you and your husband," Moore said.

"You can't do that. That's my private phone, you have no right to go snooping on it!"

"You gave us the phone voluntarily, Mrs Ward, and these messages are very relevant to our enquiry. For instance, 'I'll have the money soon, love. Just hold out a few more days.' And 'When are you going to do it?'. When was he going to do what, Mrs Ward?"

"I think I need a solicitor, please," Sheila Ward said, looking a lot less confident.

* * *

The duty solicitor was duly summoned, and the interview resumed when he was in place and had had thirty minutes to confer with his client.

"Now, what have you to say about these messages we found on your phone, Mrs Ward?" Moore asked.

"I'm not satisfied that Mrs Ward's phone was obtained legally, Inspector. I suggest that you don't pursue that line of enquiry. It would almost certainly be inadmissible in any case," the solicitor said. He was a mean, undernourished-looking man with terribly bad breath and glasses that were simply too big for his face.

"If you could just answer the question, please, Mrs Ward," Moore said, undeterred by the intervention.

Ward looked at her advocate, who shook his head slightly from side to side.

When she looked back at Moore, she had tears in her eyes.

"It was all Peter's idea. Honestly, I had nothing to do with it."

"What exactly was Peter's idea, Mrs Ward?"

"The car accident."

"I'd strongly advise you say nothing further, Mrs Ward," the wiry solicitor said.

"Can you explain for us please?" Moore said.

"When Jim was killed, Peter knew that Brenda would be coming into big money. He knows about these things.

It was he that hatched the plan to kill off Brenda, and then all that money would come to me, or should I say us?"

"But you and Peter are separated. I thought you didn't get on."

"After I had finished the affair with Jim – that's what caused Peter and I to break up in the first place – we got back together again. I never really loved anyone else but Peter, and he felt the same."

"What about his younger model you told us he had taken up with?" Burke said.

"I made that up."

Burke and Moore exchanged glances.

"Brenda found out about me and Jim, and she was really nasty about it. She threatened me and said she would get even, and she could be very spiteful. I was kind of glad when Peter suggested that he should deal with her. But I played no part in it, I swear."

"What did you know of his plan? After all there's a message here sent on the day she died that just says 'done!'. You must have known about what Peter had planned," Burke said.

"He just told me he would take care of things. He wasn't specific at all. I had no idea he was going to cause that accident. Did she suffer much?" Sheila Ward said, finding some fresh tears from somewhere.

Burke nodded at Moore, who left the room.

"Mrs Ward, I'll need you to make a full statement about what you have just told us. You may be charged with aiding and abetting, or accessory to murder, that's not up to me. We will arrest you in any case, and release you on Garda bail for the moment till I have a chance to consult with the superintendent here."

"I trust Mrs Ward's cooperation with this unfortunate matter will be taken into account, Inspector?" the solicitor said.

Burke didn't reply. He signalled to the uniformed Garda who was standing at the door to come forward and record Ward's statement, and he too left the room.

Chapter Thirty-Six

Outside the Garda station, Moore had summoned two uniformed officers and a marked squad car when Burke arrived down.

"Don't you think you'd better ask Amy to go with you?" she asked. "It was her who got the video evidence that will almost certainly nail the bastard."

"Yes, you're right. I didn't think. Can you go back upstairs and ask her to come down?"

"Sure. I take it you don't want me as well."

"No, two of us should be fine. I'll take the two uniformed officers as well though. Thanks."

* * *

Burke and Sutton drove out in convoy with the squad car containing the two uniformed Gardaí to Naas, and pulled in at the Power Electronic Devices building on the industrial estate.

Burke got out of the car and went over to the other officers.

"Just stay outside till I call you in. I want you to take his office computer and mobile phone back to town, and of course the man himself. I'll be arresting him on suspicion of murder," Burke said.

"Do you want him handcuffed, sir?" one of the young men said.

"That shouldn't be necessary. But I don't want him stopping off anywhere on the way, or making contact with anyone. He can call a solicitor when we have him in custody."

"Right. We'll wait here then."

Once inside, Burke asked the receptionist to call Peter Ward to come out from his office. When he appeared, Burke moved forward till he was facing the man at close quarters.

"Mr Peter Ward, I am arresting you on suspicion of the murder of Brenda Farrelly. You don't have to say anything, but anything you do say may be taken down in writing and used in evidence. I'd like you to come with me now please, and I need you to give me your mobile phone."

Peter Ward remained cool, although his pallor was ashen.

"This is ridiculous. How could I possibly have had anything to do with Brenda's death. You're making a big mistake here, Inspector."

"Please just come along, sir. If I need to handcuff you and carry out a search of your person, I have every right to do so."

"This is outrageous. I'll be suing you for wrongful arrest, at least."

Burke nodded to Amy Sutton who was standing behind her. She went back outside and called the two uniformed Gardaí into the building.

"Your phone please, Mr Ward," Burke said, stony-faced.

Ward reached into his jacket pocket and produced the item, handing it over reluctantly.

When the two Gardaí came inside, Burke asked them to collect Ward's office PC, bag it up, and bring it with them.

The receptionist, who had remained silent, but was horrified at the proceedings, finally spoke up.

"What do you want me to do, Mr Ward?" she said.

"Just call the solicitor and get him to meet me at the Garda station. Which one are you taking me to?"

"Store Street," Burke said.

Ward was escorted out of the building and placed in the back of the squad car, where Amy Sutton stood nearby making sure that he had no opportunity to make a run for it. When the uniformed officers had collected Ward's PC and placed it in the boot of the Hyundai, they all set off again back towards the city.

* * *

Back in Store Street, Burke and Sutton waited for the arrival of Ward's solicitor.

"How do you want to play this, boss?" Sutton asked as they sat in Burke's office over a cup of coffee and a sandwich apiece.

"Head on, Amy. I'll tell him about his wife's statement, and we'll be able to get messages off his phone. Can you get that to forensics and get them working on it?"

"Yes, sure."

"I doubt if he'll come clean, but it doesn't matter. We have enough to charge him with murder in any case. Before we go in, I'll just run it past the Super to make sure he's happy about it. Give me twenty minutes, then we'll get started."

* * *

Burke was back after ten minutes, and Amy Sutton joined him to start the interview with Peter Ward.

Ward's solicitor was a woman whom Burke judged to be in her early forties. She was dressed in a business trouser suit, and her hair was very well styled. Her makeup was applied carefully and sparingly, and she sported a Mont Blanc pen and a yellow legal pad. She introduced herself as Marian McGough in an accent that placed her north of Dublin, possibly from County Louth, Burke thought.

The four of them settled down in the room where Ward and McGough were on one side of the small rectangular table, and the two Gardaí were on the other.

"Mr Ward, I'd like you to tell us a little about your relationship with Sheila Ward, if you will," Burke said.

"No comment," came the reply in an even, but disinterested tone.

Burke looked at Sutton, and they exchanged a slightly concerned glance.

"Very well. Perhaps then you can tell us about your company. What types of electronic device do you specialize in?"

"No comment."

"I see. Mr Ward, I should point out that your refusal to cooperate will not go well for you when this matter comes to court, as it surely will."

"No comment."

Burke then produced an evidence bag in which the device that had been removed from Brenda Farrelly's car was clearly visible.

"Mr Ward, please look at this and tell me if you recognize it at all," he said, pushing the item across the table towards the man.

Ward barely glanced at the device.

"No comment."

"Mr Ward, this will do you now good at all. We have a statement that clearly implicates you in the murder of Brenda Farrelly. Furthermore, we have CCTV evidence that places you at or near the scene of her car crash at the time of her death. We have evidence that you intended to share the proceeds of the Farrellys' estate, perhaps not in equal measure, with Sheila Ward. So, there's no point in refusing to answer my questions, you see. You're not doing yourself any favours."

McGough leaned in a little towards Burke.

"Inspector, I think my client had made it clear that he has no intention of answering any of your questions, so I think it would be best if you do whatever you have to do and end this interview."

"What I have to do, Ms McGough, is to charge your client with murder. Then he will be brought to the Circuit Court later today and I can assure you we will be opposing bail."

"And on what basis will you be attempting to deny my client his legal rights?"

"On the basis that he may attempt to interfere with witnesses. And it is a very serious charge, after all."

"That's as may be, Inspector, but I'm not satisfied that you have sufficient, or even any, evidence to proceed with a murder charge against my client."

"Fortunately, it is not you that I have to satisfy in that regard, Ms McGough. If your client is not prepared to assist us, then we will do as you suggest and charge him. Amy, would you bring Mr Ward to the front desk and have him charged please?"

"Yes, sir. Come along with me please, sir," Sutton said, standing up.

Amy Sutton, Marian McGough and Peter Ward went outside to the custody sergeant and Ward was charged. Again, he said nothing, other than to confirm that he understood the charge.

"What time do you expect to bring Mr Ward before the court, Inspector?" McGough said.

"If you give me your mobile number, I'll let you know."

"Right," she said, handing over a business card.

Chapter Thirty-Seven

It was after five o'clock on Thursday when Burke brought everyone together for a briefing on their activity for the following day. Andrea Bergin had called him earlier, but he had not taken the call. He assumed she was hoping to set something up for them for the coming weekend, but given developments, that was the last thing he wanted.

"Right, everyone. Let's get this done. Dónal, can you arrange four uniformed officers to meet us at the airport tomorrow at 7:30 a.m.? Inform the Airport Police what's going on, but I want our own men with us for this one. We'll arrange their disguise when we get there. I don't want anyone in the airline tipping the crew off."

"OK, boss. I'll make sure we have the manpower," Lawler said.

"Good. Now, here's the plan. Fiona and I will hang around the arriving aircraft when it gets in from Gatwick. We'll be in high-vis outfits too, so we shouldn't stand out. When all the passengers are off, I'll go up the front steps while Fiona guards the rear steps with two of the uniforms in case anyone makes a dash for it. I'll arrest Marta and the co-pilot with the help of the other two uniforms and we'll bring them back here. I want the aircraft sealed and searched then. If there are significant quantities of drugs on board, we want to find them, and God knows where they may have them stashed. Is everyone clear?"

The team nodded and mumbled their assent.

"What do you want Dónal and I to do, boss?" Amy Sutton asked.

"Oh, don't worry, Amy. I want you out there too. You can keep an eye on the rest of the ground crew, and when I've taken the women off, I'd like you to body search the pilot. We have no evidence to suggest that he is involved, but better to be sure than sorry. Search his big pilot's bag, but don't be too heavy-handed unless he cuts up rough."

"Right, sir," Sutton said.

"Fine. Fiona, let's meet here at 6:45 a.m. tomorrow and we'll get out there nice and early. The traffic at the airport roundabout can be a bit busy at that time with all the early morning departures, so best to go in a marked car."

"Right, boss," Moore said.

"OK, everyone, that's it for now. Till tomorrow then," Burke said, dismissing the team.

As he made his way back to his office, Fiona Moore asked him, "Boss, can I have a word?"

"Sure, Fiona, come in."

When they were both in Burke's office, he gestured for her to sit down.

"What's on your mind?" he said.

"Do you think this is a good idea, sir?" Moore said, a little tentatively.

"Do I think what is a good idea?"

"You know. You arresting Andrea Bergin."

"And why would that not be a good idea, Sergeant?"

Moore could see that he wasn't going to make this easy for her.

"Well, I just thought, what with your relationship with her, it could be a bit tricky, that's all."

Burke remained silent for a few moments.

"Sergeant, not that it's any of your business, but I am quite capable of doing my job as a police officer without your interference. My 'relationship', as you call it, with Bergin, will not affect me carrying out my duties, of that you can be assured. Is there anything else on your mind?"

"Eh, no, sir, nothing."

"Good. Then till tomorrow," he said, and looked down at his desk where he started to read some paperwork that had been left for him.

* * *

It was a dull, misty morning the following day when the team assembled in Store Street. Burke and Moore requisitioned a marked car, while Sutton and Lawler went ahead in Lawler's VW Passat. The four uniformed Gardaí, who had been briefed about their mission, were in another marked car, and the convoy set off at a brisk pace towards the airport.

"See if you can get the Gatwick flight up on FlightRadar on your phone, Fiona," Burke said as they sped through the very light traffic of the early morning out along Dorset Street towards Glasnevin. "I don't want any surprises this morning."

"It hasn't left yet, boss. But it's not due to take off for a little while anyway."

"OK, well, keep an eye on that thing for it, will you?"

"Yes, sure."

The traffic at the airport roundabout was, as Burke had predicted, heavy. There were what seemed like dozens of taxis, as well as several buses and a large number of private cars. Burke put on the blue lights and siren on the squad car, and although some drivers were slow to get out of the way, they got past the jam reasonably quickly.

After a few minutes, they arrived at Terminal 1, parked the car directly outside and went in.

Inside the airport, the four of them along with the other four Gardaí collared a European Airways despatcher and established the gate number where the inbound flight from Gatwick would arrive. Using their Garda IDs they pushed their way past security, and got to gate D108 quickly.

Once at the gate, they made themselves known to the staff who were manning the gate in preparation for the departure to Gatwick. Even at this stage, a number of passengers had started to collect around the gate itself, awaiting the arrival of the incoming plane.

"Where is it now, Fiona?" Burke said.

Moore consulted her phone again, and said, "Just coming up over the Irish Sea. It has started to descend. It's at 14,000 feet, estimating twelve minutes to landing, but this app is often a bit optimistic with the timings."

"OK."

Burke turned to the team.

"Right, everyone, time to take up out positions. This chap here has your yellow vests. Put them on and try to look like airport workers."

The European Airways man overseeing the departure gate let them through, and they filed down the stairs, and out onto the apron. It was cold and damp outside, but they hardly noticed.

They all stayed close to the building until another European Airways despatcher pointed to a Boeing 737 just touching down on runway 28.

"Here's your Gatwick service now, Inspector," he said. "Do you want us to do anything different?"

"No. Just act as normal. We'll do the necessary."

"Righto," the man said, not knowing quite what to expect.

As the aircraft turned in off the taxiway and slowly approached the docking area, the noise from its engines was quite deafening. But then as the nose of the aircraft dipped briefly and the machine came to a halt, they were switched off, and they wound down slowly.

"Yes, please, but let me get a few more men to go with us. We don't want her slipping away again!"

On Burke's instructions, relayed via the European Airways despatcher, the door of EI-SND was opened and the stairs lowered onto the taxiway. Burke ascended the steps followed by two uniformed Gardaí, and found Andrea Bergin still strapped into her seat in the front row of the plane.

"We meet again," Burke said. "Not nice, Andrea, not nice at all. Now this time I'm going to have to handcuff you. C'mon now, don't make it any harder than it has to be."

Bergin started to sob quietly as Burke put the cuffs on her thin wrists.

* * *

The team regrouped inside the terminal building in a room that had been provided by the ever-helpful airline.

"Forensics have arrived, boss, and they're going over the plane now. We found four baggies of white powder in Marta's tunic. It's almost certainly cocaine. And I lifted Bergin's big black flight bag too and had a nosey in it. I found another twenty baggies in there. Must be worth over a grand. I've given it to forensics to swab and record the evidence," Dónal Lawler said.

"Nice work, Dónal. Anything on the pilot, Kaan?"

"No, sir. Squeaky clean. He may have known something of what was going on, but I'd say he didn't want to get involved."

Just then, a forensics officer dressed in a white paper scene-of-crime suit knocked on the door and came in. She pulled down her hood to reveal a full head of red hair tied off in a ponytail.

"Sorry to butt in, folks, but I thought you might like to know about this," she said, holding up a small transparent plastic container.

"What's that then?" Burke said.

"I'm not sure, but it looks deadly to me. I'll need to have it properly analysed, of course, but it's not cocaine, that's for sure. We've tested for that already. I'll get it off to the lab as soon as possible."

"Thanks, and be sure to let me know as soon as you have a result, won't you?" Burke said.

"Yes, of course, sir."

"European Airways won't be too pleased with us," Burke said, smiling. "It's the second time we've buggered up their schedule. Anyway, never mind. Let's get back into town. I want to have a word with those two before they get all lawyered up on us."

* * *

On the way back to the city, Moore, who was travelling in Burke's car, said, "Listen, boss. Are you sure you wouldn't like me to question Bergin? I have a feeling she's going to try and use whatever there has been between you to wriggle out if this whole thing, or at least compromise the investigation."

Burke thought for a minute before replying.

"Maybe you're right, Fiona. I'm going to have to tell the Super in any case, and I may not even survive that. He may bust me down to sergeant again and send me to bloody Kerry!"

"Or maybe even the Aran Islands, boss!"

They both laughed out loud.

Chapter Thirty-Nine

When they got to town, Burke went upstairs to find the superintendent and advise him of developments. Dónal Lawler was assigned to interview Marta Dudek, as Fiona Moore wanted to have a go at Bergin.

Lawler brought Amy Sutton with him to interview the Polish cabin attendant.

Marta was in her work uniform, and looked incongruous seated in the small interview room, but nevertheless, quite relaxed.

Lawler had the small bags of cocaine that had been removed when she was searched during the arrest. He placed them on the table between them.

"How long have you known Andrea Bergin, Marta?" he said, using the age-old technique of starting with easy questions.

Marta shrugged before answering. She was clearly not in a chatty mood, and Lawler sensed she was a little frightened by her current circumstances.

"How long, Marta?" Lawler persisted.

"Just over two years, I suppose."

"And how long have you been selling drugs on board?"

"Will I be sent back to Poland? You know I will be killed if you send me back."

"Why would anyone want to do that, Marta?"

"Simple. To stop me giving evidence. That's what they do."

"That's what who do, Marta?"

"I can't say. They will kill me. They are ruthless."

"No, Marta, I don't think you will be sent back to Poland. But you will be brought to court here in Ireland charged with supplying class A drugs. You will almost certainly face a prison sentence."

The girl put her hand to her face, and sobbed quietly, turning her head away from the two Gardaí.

"But that's not really what we are interested in, Marta," Amy Sutton said.

Marta looked at Sutton with a quizzical look on her face.

"No. You see, the drugs are a done deal. It just depends on what humour the judge is in when you appear in court, and how much of the stuff we can find amongst your things. But what we are really interested in is the murder of Jim Farrelly on board one of your aeroplanes," Sutton said.

"How do you mean?"

"I think you know very well what we mean, Marta. A powerful and very deadly poison was administered to Mr Farrelly on the morning he flew to Gatwick with European Airways. A flight on which you were the senior cabin attendant. What can you tell us about that?"

"I don't know anything about that," Marta said.

"Just now, Marta, we have recovered the box in which we believe the fatal dose was stored. We found it in Andrea's flight bag. It's with our forensic people right now, and if we find your fingerprints or any traces of your DNA on it, then you will be charged with murder. And that, Marta, is a totally different matter altogether."

"I can't say anything. They will kill me."

Lawler decided to try another approach.

"Marta, maybe we could do something here. If you were to tell us all about Mr Farrelly, and what part you played in his killing, we might be able to do something for you in relation to the various charges," Lawler said.

"What do you mean?"

"Well, I'd have to talk to my boss about it. But, as I said, we're not too bothered about the drugs. The Swedish police are working on that, and we probably won't get too involved. It's the murder we are keen to solve. After all, the man was a completely innocent Irishman."

"What can you do for me?" Marta said.

"I don't know yet. I need to speak to someone. I'll be back shortly," Lawler said, nodding to Amy Sutton, and both of them left the room.

* * *

Superintendent Jerome Heffernan was not in a good humour when Inspector Aidan Burke came into his office.

"Come in, Aidan. Sit," he barked.

Burke took a seat opposite the big man, who glowered at him from across a clean desk.

"What the fuck is going on, Aidan? I've had the boss of European Airways on the phone giving out stink about you and your team freezing not one, but two of their planes, not to mention hauling their crew off in handcuffs. Would you care to explain?"

Burke filled his boss in on what exactly had taken place while Heffernan listened intently.

"And what's all this I hear about you and the pilot woman? For God's sake, Aidan, don't tell me you've been thinking with your dick!"

"No, sir. It's not like that. We did have a very brief relationship, but it's over now, and it won't stop me dealing with her objectively, I can assure you."

"Jesus, Aidan, if the press get hold of this, you'll be out on your ear, and I won't be able to save your ass."

"I know, sir. I'm sorry. But I think it's all manageable, if I could just get on and do the interviews."

"No chance. You don't go anywhere near that woman. Is that understood? Now, I mean it, Aidan. In fact, it might be better if you took a few days off," Heffernan said.

"I hear what you're saying, sir, but I think it really needs me to wrap this all up neatly. I promise I won't have anything to do with Andrea Bergin."

"You'd better not. How near are we to charging someone with something anyway?"

"Very close, sir. I expect to be charging Marta Dudek and Andrea Bergin later today. And don't forget we've already dealt with Peter Ward. He's been charged."

"Yes, I remember. I suppose that's something. But listen, when we were talking before, you said you thought that this Farrelly's killing was work-related – something to do with a pharmaceutical company he was involved with. How come all of a sudden it's something else entirely?"

"We're just following the evidence, sir. There may well be something dodgy about his client, AMRAAL, but there's no evidence to suggest that it got him killed."

"Hmph. Right, well get on with it then. And let's pray that you can wrap this whole thing up without anyone leaking to the press. And keep me informed, OK?"

"Thank you, sir. Yes of course."

"And, Aidan. No more messing about now, do you hear? If you need some female company, try and avoid murder suspects!"

"Yes, sir."

Heffernan looked down and started shuffling the few papers on his desk, a signal that the meeting was over.

Chapter Forty

When Burke returned to his office, he was keen to find out how the interviews were going. He didn't have to wait long. He had no sooner sat down, when Dónal Lawler came in.

"Hi, Dónal. What's the craic?" Burke said.

"I'm dealing with the stewardess, Marta Dudek. She's quite scared. She thinks we're going to deport her to Poland and, she says, if that happens her life will be in danger. But she's keeping shtum about the other business. Any ideas?"

"Yes, I have. Here's what we'll do."

* * *

Lawler found Amy Sutton in the open plan having a much-needed cup of coffee.

"C'mon, Amy, let's get this thing wrapped up."

Amy Sutton was a bit mystified by her colleague's comment, but she wasn't about to argue.

On the way downstairs, Lawler filled her in. The two of them returned to the interview room where Marta Dudek was waiting nervously.

"Right, Marta. As you suspected, the senior officers are indeed talking about deportation. I don't know if I can persuade them to keep you here. That depends on you."

"I don't understand. What do you mean?" Marta said.

"Well, if you were able to tell us exactly what went on with Mr Farrelly, I might be able to persuade them to keep you here on just the drug charges, depending on what you tell us."

Marta sobbed some more.

"Look, Marta, I know you're in a very difficult position here. But you don't have a lot of choices. Why not work with us? We can make things better for you if you cooperate. And if you were acting under duress, that will help your case too," Amy Sutton said.

"OK. But you must promise me about the deportation," Marta said.

"We can't make promises, Marta, but if you tell us exactly what happened, it will certainly help you. I can promise you that," Lawler said.

"OK, OK. I did put the tablet that Andrea gave me into his drink on the morning flight. I didn't know what it was, or what it would do to him. She just told me that I had to do it, because the passenger had been recording information about our business. Andrea gave me the box with the tablet in it and told me not to touch it – just to empty it into his cup and pour the coffee in on top of it. Then I had to give the pill box back to Andrea and wash my hands. So, I did it."

"Are you sure you didn't know what was in the tablet?"

"No, of course I didn't."

"What did you think it contained?"

"I didn't know. Maybe just something to make him sick, like a warning or something. I just did what I was told."

"Tell me, Marta, who organizes the drugs for you to sell on board?" Sutton said.

"Andrea does. She gets the drugs from her contact in Stockholm. She is able to bring it on board, because no one searches her flight bag at security. Then she passes it out to me when the plane is on the ground."

"Are any of the other crew involved?" Sutton said.

"No. We keep the business between us."

"How much do you make in a week, Marta?"

"It varies. But usually three or four thousand euro. Andrea takes 70% of the money, and I get 30%. She has to pay for the drugs."

"How long has this been going on, Marta?" Lawler asked.

"Over a year."

"OK. Well, we need to ask you to make an official statement. Then you will be charged with supply, and you will be taken before a judge."

"And the deportation?" Marta said.

"That's not up to me, but I will tell them upstairs that you have been helpful to us."

Lawler left Amy Sutton to oversee the taking of the statement, and went looking for Fiona Moore.

* * *

Moore felt quite uncomfortable as she sat down opposite Andrea Bergin in the interview room at Store Street Garda station. She would very much liked to have Aidan Burke with her, as was their usual practice when interviewing a suspect in a case of serious crime, but of course in this instance it was out of the question. She decided on the direct approach.

"What can you tell me about the death of Jim Farrelly, Ms Bergin?"

"Oh, I see. You're aware, of course, that I have had an affair with your boss Aidan, Fiona. What is it? A little jealous, are we? Would you have liked to have been between the sheets with the inspector instead of me? Is that it?"

"Just answer the question, please," Moore said, but she was aware that her face had flushed a little, and she cursed inwardly to herself.

"I'm not going to answer any of your questions, Detective. Bring me the organ grinder, and I'll talk to him, or maybe we'll just make love right here in the room. You can stay and watch if you like. What do you say?" Bergin said with a mischievous grin.

"Ms Bergin, I'm not sure you understand the seriousness of the situation. We have a statement that clearly implicates you in the killing of a passenger on one of your flights. We have forensic evidence linking you to the method by which he was killed. So, you see, we have every reason to charge you with murder. It would be best for you if you just answered my questions, and cut out the drama."

Andrea Bergin sat back in her chair and gave an artificial laugh.

"You don't get it, do you, Sergeant. Aidan said you were a bit slow. All I have to do is make a single phone call to the local papers here and mention how a senior officer in the Gardaí was bedding a murder suspect and using his position to intimidate me, and it's game over for you two."

Bergin leaned forward across the table, so that she was close to Fiona Moore's face.

"What you need to do is let me out of here and drive me back to the airport so I can fly away out of this dump and get on with my life. Right?"

"Wrong, Ms Bergin. Just stay where you are for a few minutes. I'll be right back."

Moore left the room and went in search of Burke who was in his office.

"Hi," she said, "how did it go with Heffernan?"

"Apart from the fact that he tore the arse out of me, not too bad. What's the story downstairs?"

Moore told Aidan Burke what had transpired between herself and Andrea Bergin.

"I see. Well, if that's the way she wants to play it, I have a plan. But I'll need to run it past Heffernan. Oh, and what was the name of that police officer you were dealing with in Sweden?"

"Lundqvist, Klara Lundqvist. Why do you ask?"

"I think it might be time for some European cooperation. Can you give her a call while I'm up with himself and see if she has anything to say about things there?"

"Yes, OK. But what have you got in mind?"

"You'll see."

Moore went off to call Sweden while Burke went upstairs to get sanction for whatever plan he had in mind. They met up back in Burke's office ten minutes later.

"Well?" Burke said.

"It's gas. They've arrested eight of the gang over there, and recovered several kilos of cocaine and lots of cash. Four of them work for airlines and the others are involved in the supply. She says they won't get near the people at the top of the food chain, but they have enough to disrupt their operation for a while in any case. How did you get on upstairs?"

"Grand. Come with me."

Chapter Forty-One

When Burke and Moore entered the interview room where Andrea Bergin was waiting, Bergin got up and walked towards the inspector.

"Ah, Aidan, love, I was wondering if you would come to my rescue."

She went to embrace him, but Burke pushed her away roughly and told her to sit down.

"I see. You've changed your attitude then. Or is this just to impress little Fiona here?" Bergin said, looking at Moore.

"In about two minutes, Ms Bergin, I'm going to take you outside and have you charged with conspiracy to murder. You will be found guilty, and you will spend between eight and ten years in the Bridewell where you will no doubt be much admired by your fellow inmates, and maybe even some of the screws. So, unless you stop messing around and start talking, your flying days are well and truly over."

Bergin sat down again and remained silent for a few minutes, contemplating her position.

"All right, I'll tell you. But I want a deal."

"You tell us what you know, and then we'll see what we can do based on the information you provide."

"Think of it as a business, Aidan. A big business. We have the supply side, which mostly involves shipping the stuff from Colombia; the storage and distribution side, which takes place at locations in Sweden, the Netherlands, Germany and Lithuania; and then the retail side. The stuff is eventually sold to willing buyers on board several different airlines' flights, to airport workers, customs officials and others. It's a very well-oiled operation and generates many millions of euros in revenue every year. But because the operation involves contraband, the organizers have to be very ruthless if they think it is going to be compromised in any way. Hence, poor Mr Farrelly."

"How do you mean?"

"He was observed recording what we were doing – selling snow on board. And he was a lawyer as well. He represented a serious risk to the organisation. When information about him got back up the line, it was decided he had to be taken out. So, he was. It's not the first time we have had to see someone off to protect the business. I was given a tablet to be administered on board, and Marta slipped it into his drink on the early morning flight to Gatwick. It was just bad luck that it eventually killed him later on the return flight. If he had got home safely and died the following day or something, I wouldn't be here now."

Moore could hardly believe the coldness of the woman as she told her story.

"Maybe not. What about the supply side of this business you describe?"

"Ah. I get my supplies locally in Stockholm. They are left for me at a secure drop-off. When you were enjoying your *petite mort* after you made love to me, I went off and collected a package and put it in the boot of my car. You never suspected a thing."

Burke shuffled uneasily in his seat.

"OK. Names then. We need to know who your contacts are. That's the only way we can help you," Burke said.

"No chance. If I told you that I might as well kill myself. These people don't mess around."

Burke looked at Moore.

"Tell me, Andrea, how much money have you made out of this little business of yours over the past, say, two years?" Moore said.

"More than you will earn in a lifetime, Sergeant. Ask Aidan to tell you about my apartment and my car. He's been in both," Bergin said.

"And are any of the other crew on board, apart from Marta, involved in this business, Andrea?" Burke said.

"No. They may have an idea that there's something going on, but they are not in on it. Having too many involved dilutes the profit and risks leakage. Are you going to charge me then?"

"Don't be in such a rush, Andrea. All in good time. Have you anything more to tell us at all about this operation that could help your position?" Moore said.

"I can't say anything more. Better to be alive in prison than dead at the side of the road, don't you think?"

Burke nodded to Moore and the two of them got up and left the room.

* * *

Upstairs, when Moore and Burke were back in his office, Moore said, "What's your plan, then?"

"Fancy a trip to Sweden?" Burke said.

"What?"

"The boss has been onto the Swedish police. He called Lundqvist. Bergin's going back home, but in handcuffs. We get to keep Dudek. That's the deal."

"Christ, Aidan, are you serious?"

"Very. Heffernan wants Bergin gone so she can't stir up trouble with the media here. If she tells her story about me and her in Sweden, no one will be the slightest bit interested, and the Swedish authorities will charge her with conspiracy to murder, as well as all the drugs business. We'll supply the evidence we have, and we'll probably have to go over there for her trial, unless she pleads guilty, which I think she will, by the way."

"I take it she's not going back on European Airways?"

"Correct. There's an SAS flight to Stockholm tomorrow morning and they'll take Bergin and two officers out on it. Fancy it?"

"No. I don't. And while we're at it, did you tell blondie that I was dumb?"

"What! No, of course not. Why would I say that?"

"Maybe because you think it, boss."

"Look, Fiona, that's rubbish. I admire you. I rely on you all the time. We work really well together. I often think you're smarter than I am. She's just trying to wind you up."

"OK, for now, I suppose. I'll arrange for a couple of plain clothes officers to escort her tomorrow, and I'll tidy up the Marta Dudek thing as well. What's the charge? Conspiracy to murder?"

"Yes, and possession of class A with intent to supply. Thanks. I'd better call Mitchell in the solicitor's place and tell him that Farrelly's death was not connected to any of their clients. That should please him."

Epilogue

Andrea Bergin flew out the following morning on the SAS flight. She was discretely handcuffed under a coat to two plain clothes Garda officers, and they were seated in the front row of the aircraft surrounded by empty seats. When they arrived at Stockholm, the plane was met by Lundqvist and a small battery of Swedish police, and Bergin was released from the handcuffs and taken away in a Swedish police car that had been parked at the foot of the plane's steps. As predicted, she pleaded guilty to the charges that were brought against her, and remained tight-lipped about her associates in the drug business. She was sentenced to fourteen years.

Marta Dudek was brought to court. It was several months before her trial, and she was remanded in custody in the meantime. As the trial approached, her defence lawyers entered into serious negotiations with the DPP, and she pleaded guilty to the lesser charge of aiding and abetting as well as possession. She was handed down a sentence of three years for each offence, to run concurrently, and under the Irish system that meant that she would serve just two years. The Gardaí hoped that her time in prison would be sufficient to make her change her ways.

Peter Ward was tried for conspiracy to murder his sister-in-law Brenda Farrelly. He was given an eight-year sentence, with the last year suspended in recognition of his guilty plea. Power Electronic Devices went into liquidation, its bank and some trade creditors suffering the brunt of the associated losses. The DPP decided that it would not be in their best interests to charge Sheila Ward. The evidence against her was very thin, and they reckoned that a decent defence barrister would probably get her off on the basis of coercion or duress in any case. She donated a large part of the money she had inherited from her sister to charity, and a line was drawn under the matter.

Milligan Walker smoothed over the loss of their partner with AMRAAL, and continue to represent the company to this day. Trebutivan is now manufactured in Ireland, and much of the chatter in the medical press about possible serious side effects has died down. The company is contemplating a big expansion of its Irish facility to bring another life-saving drug to market.

Burke had to work hard to overcome the shadow that hung over his reputation and career as a result of his liaison with Andrea Bergin. Heffernan came down quite hard on him, and sought all sorts of assurances that he would behave differently in future. But the story never did reach the media, for which all concerned were very grateful. Burke had some fence-mending to do with his sergeant too. It took time, but after they had worked a few more tricky cases, the relationship settled down.

Character List

DI Aidan Burke – a tough, and sometimes rough, member of An Garda Síochána with a rather barren love life.

Sergeant Fiona Moore – a clever detective who works with Burke and sometimes outsmarts him.

Dónal Lawler – a diligent member of the detective team in Store Street Garda station.

Amy Sutton – a junior detective that shows a lot of promise.

Aileen Brophy – pathologist.

Daniel – a forensic officer who loves technology and is good with his hands.

Klara Lundqvist – a Swedish Detective Inspector.

Captain Piotr Kaan – a pilot with European Airways.

Andrea Bergin – an attractive Swedish co-pilot with an interesting side-line.

Marta Dudek – a senior cabin attendant with European Airways.

Sally, Elena and Nikolina – cabin crew with European Airways.

Rory Dillon – a flight despatcher with European Airways.

Jim Farrelly – a Dublin-based solicitor with some interesting clients.

Brenda Farrelly – wife of Jim Farrelly.

Miriam Clarke – Jim Farrelly's PA.

Sheila Ward – Brenda Farrelly's sister.

Peter Ward – Sheila's estranged husband, runs an electronics factory in Naas, County Kildare.

Kendron Mitchell – practice manager at Milligan Walker, Solicitors, Dublin.

Breffni Wagstaff – runs the London office of Milligan Walker.

Joe Byrne and Mary Looney – crew schedulers at European Airways.

If you enjoyed this book, please let others know by leaving a quick review on Amazon. Also, if you spot anything untoward in the paperback, get in touch. We strive for the best quality and appreciate reader feedback.

editor@thebookfolks.com

www.thebookfolks.com

OTHER BOOKS BY DAVID PEARSON

In this series:

A Deadly Dividend (Book 1)
A Fatal Liaison (Book 2)
The China Chapter (Book 3)
Lethal in Small Doses (Book 4)
Passion for Murder (Book 6)

In the Galway Homicides series:

Murder on the Old Bog Road (Book 1)
Murder at the Old Cottage (Book 2)
Murder on the West Coast (Book 3)
Murder at the Pony Show (Book 4)
Murder on Pay Day (Book 5)
Murder in the Air (Book 6)
Murder at the Holiday Home (Book 7)
Murder on the Peninsula (Book 8)
Murder at the Races (Book 9)
Murder in a Safe Haven (Book 10)
Murder in an Irish Bog (Book 11)
Murder in a Seaside Town (Book 12)

Available in paperback and free with Kindle Unlimited

SELECTED TITLES OF INTEREST

A woman is found in a ditch, murdered. As the list of suspects grows, an Irish town's dirty secrets are exposed. Detective Inspector Mick Hays and DS Maureen Lyons are called in to investigate. But getting the locals to even speak to the police will take some doing. Will they find the killer in their midst?

When a nurse finds a reclusive old man dead in his armchair in his cottage, the local Garda surmise he was the victim of a burglary gone wrong. However, having suffered a violent death and there being no apparent robbery, Irish detectives are not so sure. It will take all their wits and training to track down the killer.

A man is found dead during the annual Connemara Pony Show. Panic spreads through the event when it is discovered he was murdered. Detective Maureen Lyons leads the investigation but the powers that be threaten to stonewall the inquiry.

After a wealthy businessman's plane crashes into bogland it is discovered the engine was tampered with. But who out of the three occupants was the intended target? DI Maureen Lyons leads the investigation, which points to shady dealings and an even darker crime.

When a body turns up in a bog in a remote part of Ireland, the victim's brother falls under suspicion. After all, there were few others around. But why? There is clearly much more hidden beneath the sodden surface for detectives to unearth.

When a librarian and rare book dealer is shot dead in her home, Irish detectives are stumped for a motive. After suspicion falls on her gun-toting family, it will take all of their investigative powers to read between the lines and catch the killer in their midst.

www.thebookfolks.com

Made in the USA
Monee, IL
29 April 2022

95605546R00135